# LILY, WINDY AND THE WITCH

# LILY, WINDY AND THE WITCH

## THE JOURNEY BEGINS

Yvonne Carlin-Page

Illustrated by Dom McNulty

LITTLE HAVEN BOOKS

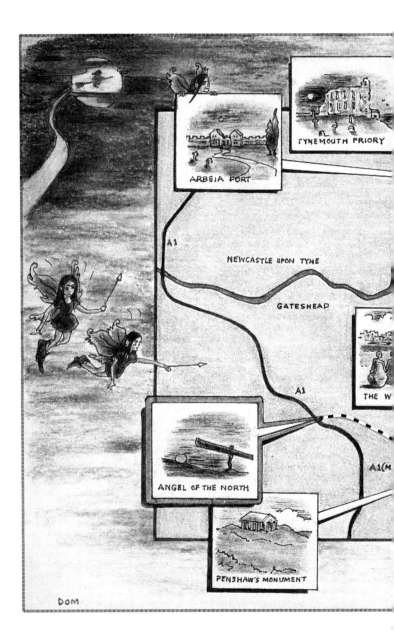

ARBEIA FORT

TYNEMOUTH PRIORY

A1

NEWCASTLE UPON TYNE

GATESHEAD

THE W

A1

A1(M

ANGEL OF THE NORTH

PENSHAW'S MONUMENT

DOM

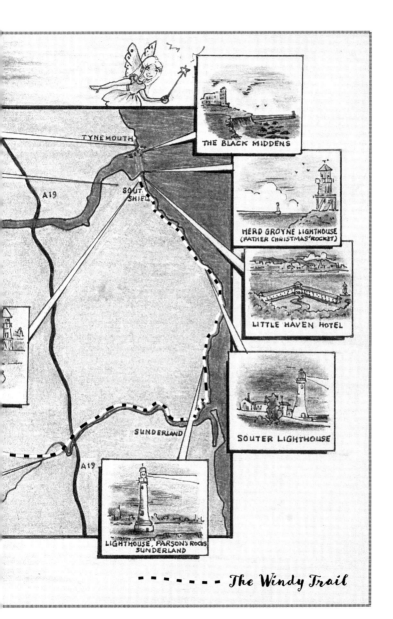

THE BLACK MIDDENS

HERD GROYNE LIGHTHOUSE
(FATHER CHRISTMAS' ROCKET)

LITTLE HAVEN HOTEL

SOUTER LIGHTHOUSE

LIGHTHOUSE, PARSON'S ROCKS
SUNDERLAND

TYNEMOUTH

SOUTH SHIELDS

A19

SUNDERLAND

A19

- - - - - - - The Windy Trail

First Published in 2016 by Little Haven Books
www.littlehavenbooks.co.uk

ISBN 978-0-9934725-0-3

A CIP record for this book
is available from the British Library

Printed and bound by
Marston Book Services Ltd
Oxfordshire

SET IN THE NORTH-EAST OF ENGLAND

# CHAPTER ONE

Lily stared up at the big pink elephant-shaped clock on her bedroom wall. 'The little hand is still on six,' she whispered, 'and the big hand is straight up. Six o' clock!' she squealed triumphantly. So it was true: Benji-bat had stopped clock-time!

Sometimes there is a noiseless night so strange and so quiet that if a bat as much as sneezes, it startles and wakes up all the other birds and animals. It was on an enchanted night like this, in the town of South Shields, at the mouth of the long and winding River Tyne in the north-east of England, a small girl opened her bedroom window and stared out wistfully. Slobberchops, a big, gangly dog with one tooth and large floppy ears, stood loyally by her side. There were lots of things Slobberchops did not like, but it would be true to say nothing much worried this good-natured dog – unless Lily was sad, or like now, in some kind of danger.

'Stop Lily. Pleeease – stop now!' His forehead creased into a big wonky frown as he yelped: 'You might fall out!'

'You stop it! I'm all right. Now shush Slobberchops,' Lily whispered urgently. 'We don't want mummy to hear us!'

Lily Bloom was up on her tiptoes, struggling to lean out of her window – and not topple out. The problem (which was always a problem) was her poorly left leg. It had a big, heavy brace clamped onto it, and she wore an even bigger black boot.

Leaning so far out of the window had made Lily feel dizzy as well as thrilled. It was just as if there was a crazy party going on inside her head! She stared up at the yellow disc hanging amongst stars sparkling like angel fire. It was a full moon, and BIG magic only happened on silent nights when the moon shone big round and beautiful – like tonight! She steadied herself, then, opening her mouth extraordinarily wide, she gulped in gallons and gallons of the crisp, clean night air. It was worth all the effort. Lily knew there was magic in this air. And she had three wishes to make.

'I wish I didn't have to wear my ugly leg brace,' she announced to a startled creature sleeping in a tree in her back garden.

'Twit-twoo,' it hooted back.

'It pinches my skin,' she added with a long, sad sigh. Swinging back her booted leg, she kicked the wall under the window. 'And I hate this boot!'

'Be careful Lily!' Slobberchops yelped, alarmed. 'Don't fall out!'

Lily had worn her leg brace and boot for as long as she could remember – which was a very long time, because she had just had her sixth birthday – so this, naturally, was always going to be her first and biggest wish.

'Twit-twoo. Twit-twooo,' the creature hooted back again, staring up at her. And it kept on hooting. Lily giggled excitedly. An owl had heard her! Squeezing her fingers tightly around the windowsill, she leaned out further still. The sound was coming from something small and black with shiny pop-eyes and huge ears. It was near the top of the tree hanging upside down! It was not an owl – it was a bat!

'Shouldn't you be squeaking or something? Only owls hoot,' Lily said, thinking out loud. Although she was used to Slobberchops talking (he made all sorts of sounds only she understood), she certainly didn't expect this creature to talk back. But a moment later that's exactly what it did. 'Twit-twoo,' the bat retorted, swinging back and forth. 'What's it got to do with you? If I'm right, and I am because I'm always right, then I can hoot if I like! And, as a matter of fact, I can talk in

9

any language – including gibberish. Little girl, can you talk gibberish?'

For one brief second Lily nearly slammed the window shut.

This was tooooo scary! She took a deep breath. 'Mummy says I do,' she answered honestly.

'Well, don't. Personally, I don't like gibberish.'

'Are you a magic creature?' Lily asked nervously.

The bat swung up and perched upright on the branch. 'Benjamin-bat, at your service. Pleased to meet you. Tell me, little girl, what is your name? And what can I do for you this starry, starry night?'

'My name is Lily Bloom,' she said, reddening. Slobberchops had been frantically licking the toes on her right foot, and now his one tooth nipped at her ankle – and he was whimpering loudly. 'Stop it, Slobberchops. I'm all right. Stop it!' Wriggling out of the window further still, she took a longer, deeper breath. 'Um … Benjamin-bat, why are you here?'

'You made a wish, didn't you? Benjamin-bat, at your service.'

'Um … actually I have three wishes,' Lily said shyly.

'No wish too big, no wish too small. Just give your local Benji-bat a call!' The bat nodded politely and then flapped his webbed wings. 'Twit-twoo. Now let me have a closer look at you.' Soaring up from the tree, the bat did an impressive loop-the-loop around the window frame before swooping down – and settled on Lily's wrist! Lily froze.

'Hmmm. You have pretty chocolate-brown hair and eyes. You are a little shy, and … oh, that's amazing! You have something quite remarkable!' The bat grinned mischievously. 'But you can't hide it from me, Lily Bloom. If I'm right, and I am because I'm always right, I can see what no-one else can!'

'Except Slobberchops,' exclaimed Lily, getting annoyed. She stared at the strange little creature clinging onto her wrist. It had a tiny, pink turned-up nose and a fur body. Its webbed wings were made of smooth layers of skin stretched over needle-thin bones, and a single hooked claw stuck out alarmingly from each wing.

Lily gasped out loud. *A vampire bat!*

The question *Have you come to suck my blood?* now raced through her mind like an electric shock, but she was too scared to ask. 'Slobberchops knows everything about me,' she blurted out defiantly. 'And he will protect me!' she added quickly.

The bat leaned over the sill and stared down at Slobberchops. 'He's a dog. In my view dogs don't count. They can't fly and they are rubbish at seeing in the dark … Unlike me!' he added with a sniff. He unfolded one silken wing. As Lily continued to watch in fascination, a tiny pink tongue shot out of his mouth

LILY GASPED OUT LOUD. **A VAMPIRE BAT!** THE QUESTION **HAVE YOU COME TO SUCK MY BLOOD?** NOW RACED THROUGH HER MIND.

and he began licking along the wing slowly, grooming himself like a cat.

Suddenly, the bat looked up. 'You, little girl,' he said, staring deep into Lily's big wide eyes, 'are quite remarkable. Lily Bloom, you have a wondrous and exceptionally beautiful mind! All children are born with beautiful minds, of course, but if I'm right, and I am because, as you now know, I'm always right, yours is exceptional. Quite exceptional.' He flapped his wings excitedly. 'And … Oh! What a surprise! That's wondrous! Remarkable, quite remarkable! There is something else wondrous inside you no-one else can see but me.' He stopped flapping his wings and stuck his tiny pink nose up in the air. 'But you will have to find that out for yourself,' he added snootily. 'Now, Lily, your second wish is …?' The bat loosened its grip and Lily began to relax.

This bat didn't want to suck her blood, after all! He was a little bit toffee-nosed. But he seemed … kind, as well as strange. 'I'm dreaming,' she whispered softly. 'This is too weird to be real!'

'Well, Lily,' the bat said, cocking his head sideways, 'your second wish is …?'

'My second wish is … I wish, I wish …' suddenly *I wish my mum would stop shouting: 'Hurry up, you lazy girl!'* flashed through her mind. But it wasn't good to make spur-of-the-moment wishes, was it? They might not turn out the way you want. Lily thought a bit more, and then she made the wish she had been wishing for a long, long time.

'I wish I had special friends who take me on magical adventures. I want our adventures to be lots of fun, like a roller-coaster ride, but most of all I want to meet a big, bad witch!'

'A big, bad witch?' the bat repeated, astonished. 'Why?'

Lily didn't want to say *Because I want to be brave.* So she simply answered shyly, 'I just do.'

'And me!' whimpered Slobberchops, frantically licking her ankle. 'Don't forget me!'

'And Slobberchops, I want him to come too.'

The bat hooted again, only this time longer and louder, like a trumpet at full blast: 'TWIT-TWOO, TOODLE-OODLE-OO!'

Lily gritted her teeth.

The bat sucked in his breath. 'With your beautiful mind,' he said softly, 'I think I already know the answer to my question, but I need to hear you say it.' His tiny pink nose twitched alarmingly as he peered deeply into her eyes again. 'Lily Bloom, do you believe in magic? I mean reeeally believe?'

'Oh, yes! I do believe in magic!' she answered, giggling. 'Especially if you make my three wishes come true! Then I'll know I'm not dreaming!'

The bat danced its way along Lily's wrist, up her arm and onto her shoulder. 'Twit-twoo, twit-twoo,' it hooted into her ear. 'Make your third wish, Lily Bloom, and this too will come true!' Seconds later, Lily's magic bat was zooming out of the window.

'Twit-twoo!' the bat hooted merrily. Doing spectacular loop-the-loops, it soared higher and higher into the night sky towards the shimmering full moon before suddenly swooping down to settle on a branch of the tree again. As Lily continued to watch entranced, the bat tucked in its webbed wings, swung upside down and shut its eyes. 'Twit-twoo. Goodnight, Lily Bloom. Goodnight, Slobberchops. Sleep tight, and don't let those little bed bugs bite!'

Lily gasped. 'I've always wanted to fly,' she said excitedly. 'I wish I could fly like you!'

That was Lily's third and final wish – but, even though she firmly and utterly and completely believed in BIG magic, something told her the wish wasn't likely to come true that same night.

'I hope the universe is listening,' she said, closing the window. Toes pointed, she slid down the wall and sat on the floor.

Snuggling up next to her, Slobberchops let out a long sigh. He had watched Lily take off her boot umpteen-thousand times, and it still made him feel shivery-sad.

Lily un-popped the thick black straps. Grabbing hold of her boot, she pulled and tugged and pulled and tugged until, finally, her foot sprung free. Then she did something she had never done before but had always wanted to do.

'Vavoom, ugly boot!' she shouted. 'Vanish!' And, grabbing hold of the boot, she held it up, aimed and threw it as hard as she could. It whizzed across the room and hit the far wall: CLONK!

'Yikes!' Slobberchops barked jumping up. 'Awesome!'

'VAVOOM, UGLY BOOT! VANISH!'
'YIKES!' SLOBBERCHOPS BARKED, JUMPING UP. 'AWESOME!'

# CHAPTER TWO

~~~~~~~~~

*L*ily stared at the big ugly L-shape. It lay on its side on the floor, still and solid. No, the really BIG magic definitely wasn't going to happen tonight.

'Don't worry, Slobberchops, I think Benji-bat might be a messenger,' she said, trying to sound cheerful. 'But he has to have a little sleep first.' Going down on all fours, she crawled across the room to her bed. Even though she had made her three wishes on a night full of magic, she wasn't feeling totally happy.

In the morning, Mummy would be cross. The leg brace had left a big black smudge on the wall. Lily would have to confess, or Mummy would give Slobberchops a smack and throw him in the dark cupboard under the stairs again. Last time Mummy was cross, Slobberchops had had to stay in there for two whole days!

'I believe in magic,' Lily whispered, pulling the bedcovers over her head. 'But please, Benji-bat, make the BIG magic happen soon.' In a whisper, she added: 'And when I meet the witch, make me brave.' As Lily shut her eyes, she wondered not for the first time if it were true when Mummy said a magpie must have stolen her real child and put 'this useless, lazy child' in her place. It wasn't true. It wasn't nice, and it made her want to cry. But what was definitely true was that Lily was nothing like her parents, in looks or anything else. Mrs Bloom was short and tubby and never stopped talking, and Mr Bloom was tall and thin and hardly said anything, except for 'Yes, dear', which he said a lot.

Lily popped her head out from under the covers. 'Are you listening, Benji-bat? Make the BIG magic happen soon!'

'Twit-twoo, toodle-oo!' he hooted back. 'If I'm right, and I am, it will all happen soon, to *you*!'

Lily jumped. It sounded almost as if Benji-bat was in her room!

'*Au revoir*, Lily and Slobberchops,' he sang merrily. 'We'll meet again, don't know where, don't know when. No wish too big, no wish too small. Just give your local Benji-bat a call!'

Lily heard a squeaky laugh, a light fluttering and then silence.

'Goodnight, Benji-bat. Goodnight, Slobberchops,' she said yawning.

'Goodnight, Lily,' Slobberchops replied happily. He jumped onto her bed and curled next to her. Nudging in closer still, he whispered, 'Lily, I have a secret to tell you.'

'What secret?'

'I don't like Benji-bat!'

'Why?'

'Well it's obvious isn't it? He doesn't like me! And he's flown away and dumped you. I think he's a batty bothersome bighead! But don't worry, Lily. I'm sure it will all come out in the wash!' he sighed, giving her cheek a big, sloppy lick.

'What a funny thing to say!' Lily said, snuggling into his soft warm fur. She lifted up one fluffy earflap. 'That's cos you're a funny sort of dog,' she whispered kindly. 'And this is a funny and very strange night' she added giggling. She kissed his forehead twice. Loud sloppy kisses that made Slobberchops sigh with delight. And then, closing their eyes, they both fell fast asleep.

'Wake up, you lazy girl. I want a word with you!' Mrs Bloom loomed over Lily's bed, a hand on each hip.

Lily sat bolt upright. But before she could say anything, her mother had started yelling again.

'You threw your boot, didn't you!' She wagged a chubby finger at the black smudge on the far wall. 'How do you expect to walk properly without your boot? You ungrateful, stupid girl. You could have broken it. You wait till I tell your father! You just wait!'

Sliding quickly under the covers, Lily hid her head under her pillow. When her mother was in a foul mood such as this, the best thing to do was vanish.

Later that same morning, Lily hobbled downstairs and into the kitchen. *At least Slobberchops didn't get the blame*, she thought. Slobberchops should have been hiding under the table, eagerly waiting for his secret breakfast. That was how every morning started. Lily thought Slobberchops was the greediest but also the best dog in the world. After all, he never shouted at her, he kept all of her most secret of secrets and he was excellent at gobbling up every tiny little bit of the yucky breakfasts (lard-smeared sandwiches and a hard boiled egg) she threw under the table when Mummy wasn't looking. But on this particular morning, Slobberchops wasn't there. Lily didn't know it then, but that was the first sign something out-of-this-world was about to happen – something that would change everything. Forever.

Slobberchops was by the back door, snuffling and pawing at the ground and whimpering excitedly.

Mrs Bloom was bent over the sink filling the kettle for tea. 'Dog wants a wee,' she said glumly.

From behind his newspaper, Mr Bloom muttered, 'Yes, dear.'

Suddenly, *whoosh*! The door swung wide open.

Slobberchops took one look at the supremely odd creature standing boldly in the doorway–and bolted between Mrs Bloom's legs. 'Aaah!' she shrieked.

Mr Bloom lowered his newspaper.

Lily's mouth dropped open.

There was an eerie silence while everyone continued to stare at the mysterious creature on the mat.

The strange creature stared back.

Lily thought she had never seen anything quite so weird or so wonderful. It was huge. It had long spindly legs, a slender neck, mysterious green eyes and, from its large pointed ears to its claws and all along its enormously long fluffy tail, its fur quivered and bristled like that of a startled hedgehog. And it was standing on their mat in the doorway, nose poked high in the air like an arrogant queen. All that was missing was a crown.

It was Mrs Bloom who broke the silence. 'What the thumpy-heck?' she gasped.

'It's an Egyptian cat – sort of,' Lily said, puzzled as well as shocked. 'I've seen something like it in my school book.'

'Of course it's a cat, you nincompoop, anyone can see that!' scoffed Mrs Bloom. 'It's not a stray …' she added, pointing. 'Just look at that fancy collar!'

Everyone's gaze focused on the stiff, white collar studded with sparkling diamonds.

Mrs Bloom's ample hips jelly-wobbled with glee. This majestic-looking creature's fur was pure white! Well – apart from those funny green eyes, she thought, frowning. But cats are clean creatures. And this spectacularly odd creature will make all the neighbours sit up and take notice! Clapping her hands together, she cried, 'We'll keep it!'

Mr Bloom opened his mouth to protest.

'Shut it!' snapped Mrs Bloom. And he did.

Slobberchops sloped off to his basket under the stairs. Climbing in slowly, he let out a long, exaggerated sigh. A cat! A big, white and weird cat was going to live here! Shocking – simply shocking! Perhaps this was all a bad dream. *I'll sleep*, he told himself. *I'll have another nap, and when I wake up again, that horrid white monster will be gone and everything will go back to normal.*

Lily couldn't stop smiling. This creature was like the queen of all cats. Even if its eyes did look a bit spooky, it looked like a clever cat. And now it was going to live with them – in their house!

That same night, when Lily hobbled up to her bedroom, the strange, white cat padded in after her.

'Go back down,' she whispered urgently. 'You can't sleep upstairs. Mummy will be cross.'

No such luck. The cat jumped up onto the windowsill, lifted its paw and slowly began to lick. *Lick. Lick. Lick.*

'You are a bad cat,' Lily said glumly. She slumped down on her bed and crossed her arms. 'You are going to get me into trouble!'

The cat's green eyes narrowed as thin as blades of grass. She peered down at Lily. 'My name,' she said in a low, growling voice, 'is Bast.'

Lily nearly jumped out of her skin. First a talking bat, and now a talking cat?! This was weird and wonderful. But mostly scary! She blurted out: 'That's a funny name.' She realised she sounded rather rude.

'Don't be impertinent, little girl! I am Bast, the Patron Saint of Cats, Females and Secrets.'

'Imper … imper …' spluttered Lily.

'Have you seen it?' Bast butted in.

'What?'

'Something odd.'

Lily stood up. She stared around her room. Shrugging her shoulders she answered innocently, 'Only you.' She didn't mean to be rude, she was just being honest.

The cat leaped down from the windowsill. Growling low, whiskers twitching menacingly, she circled Lily twice. 'Stand up properly, little girl,' she snapped. 'I want to inspect you.'

'Okay,' Lily replied quickly stiffening her back. 'But only if you promise to sleep downstairs.'

'I promise,' said Bast with a wry smile. Leaning in, she sniffed. 'Keep still, little girl,' she hissed.

Lily shivered. 'What are you doing?'

'Be quiet! I'm trying to decide.' *Sniff. Sniff. Sniff.* 'Hmmm … creamy skin. Your hair is chocolate brown, your eyes are big brown buttons and you smell sweet as fairy cakes.' She leaned back, staring. 'You are like a big cream fairy cake!'

Lily shivered again. A fairy cake? She had flinched and (when no-one was looking) cried her eyes out when the school bully, Billy Moonface, had screamed across the playground 'Look at Lily Limpy-leg!' just because she couldn't walk properly. So being called 'fairy cake' sounded nice – but still, she wasn't quite sure. In a small voice she asked, 'Is that good?'

'I said be quiet! I'm trying to decide if I can trust you.'

'Oh, you can,' Lily giggled nervously. 'Slobberchops and I are really good at keeping secrets.'

The cat leaned in closer. 'Open your mouth wide.'

'No! Why should I?'

'I need to see if the tooth fairy has been in there.'

'You are strange but …' Lily began, and then giggled nervously again. She thought: *A talking cat that believes in fairies. This has to be the most amazing thing ever!* 'I think I like you, Bast – a little bit,' she added. 'I put my tooth under the pillow and next morning it was gone. Mummy said the tooth fairy had taken it, but then she laughed and called me a silly girl, so now I don't know if I believe her.'

'You wicked, wicked girl!' shrieked Bast. Her tail lashed back and forth like a whip. 'Every time a child says they don't believe, something bad happens –

something very, very bad. Grown-ups can say it, they don't know any better, but children? Never! Never! *Never*! If children stop believing, there is no hope for your world. No hope at all.'

At that very moment, in a stream of glittering light, something small and feather-light fluttered into the bedroom. Darting around the ceiling light, it squealed, 'Oh chilly dumdum! Oh crumbling crumple cakes and buttery butter sticks! Got it wrong again. Oh drat! Oh rats! Oh no!'

Lily was so shocked, she pulled herself up onto her bed, grabbed hold of her bedcover, and pulled it up to her neck.

'Got you!' Bast shouted as she swung out at the creature with both paws – and missed.

'Wheee!' the little creature squealed plummeting down.

Lily leaned over the side of her bed. She stared at the little creature sitting on the carpet rubbing her head. It was the size of a bar of white chocolate. It had pretty delicate-looking wings folded concertina-style, and nestling between each fold, a tiny emerald green eye blinked and sparkled like a precious jewel. Its long wavy golden hair swished about like a horse's tail, and two big blue eyes stared out from under eyelashes as long as spiders' legs. And it was wearing boots: *huge* bright yellow wellington boots.

IN A STREAM OF GLITTERING LIGHT, SOMETHING SMALL AND
FEATHER-LIGHT FLUTTERED INTO THE BEDROOM.

'Oh crackle-bots! Oh corky-porky crumble cakes!'
the creature cursed, unfurling its crumpled wings.
'I've lost more fairy dust. These boots are rubbish!'
she added, glaring down at them.

Lily gazed with admiration at the creature's golden
hair and beautiful wings. 'What are you?' she asked
astonished. 'Are you a fairy?'

The little creature jumped up. 'Of course I'm a fairy!
You've seen fairies on a Christmas tree. Don't I look
like one of them?' Brushing down her little wings,
she stroked them carefully back into place. 'My name
is Windy.'

'Windy, if you are a fairy, why have you got big
yellow boots on?' It was a silly thing to ask, Lily knew
it as soon as she said it, but so were the boots. Whoever
had heard of a fairy wearing big yellow boots?

Throughout all of this conversation Bast had been
hissing. Now she exploded: 'Never mind that!' The
tip of her long tail smacked the back of Windy's
boots as she added, 'It's a fine mess you've got us
into again, Windy!'

Windy glowered at Bast. 'It's not me. It's this stupid
thing!' Reaching down, she tugged at something
deep inside her right boot. Instantly, a thin spray of
sparkling yellow dust puffed up.

Lily clapped her hands over her eyes. Last time her
bedroom carpet had got this messy, Slobberchops
had trodden in some mud. Mummy had spanked

his bottom and locked him in the cupboard under the stairs.

Windy tugged and pulled and tugged some more until, suddenly, up popped a pale yellow stick. At the very tip was a glowing star.

'Crackling crackle-bots! This stupid wand won't work,' she groaned, whacking it against Lily's bed. What happened next was a bit like biting into a sherbet sweet. The glowing star crackled and fizzed, then popped. Windy glared at it angrily. 'Stupid wally-wand!' she snapped.

'It's not the wand,' said Bast loftily. 'It's the fairy who waves it. And a fairy who can't produce magic from her wand is like a witch who can't make her broom fly: utterly pointless!'

Windy lunged at Bast with her wand – and missed.

'Oh fiddly-diddly diddlesticks to you!' she yelled. 'And you can pop your daft philosophy lesson up your tail too!'

Lily's mouth dropped open but no sound came out. What do you say when a fairy flies into your room and starts fighting with a cat?

# CHAPTER THREE

~~~~~~~~~~~~~~~~~~~

Suddenly, it was all too much. 'Stop it, you two!' Lily blurted out. 'My mummy will hear you!' Holding her poorly left leg by the knee, she clambered down from her bed. She stared at Windy, then at Bast, then back at Windy again. 'Why are you here?'

'Ignore her,' snapped Bast. Her long tail shot up like an exclamation mark. 'Her name is Lily and she smells of fairy cakes.'

Now Lily really began to panic. 'Both of you – you have to gooooo! Mummy will be coming up soon to put out my light and … and I've got to clean my teeth. And you're both going to get me into *big* trouble.'

Windy stared up at Lily. 'Are you scared of your mummy?'

'No,' Lily answered truthfully. Scared wasn't quite the right word.

'But you are scared of something, aren't you? I know you are!' Windy said, fluttering her wings excitedly. 'I'm clever! I can see right inside you where your heart is. I know when someone is shivery-scared. And you are chilly-chum-wriggle-tum-shivery-scared of something, aren't you?'

Lily nodded. It didn't make any difference whether her eyes were open or closed, horrid Billy Moonface was always there, scaring her. Bast and Windy were scary. But that was the jumpy what's-going-to-happen-next? sort, which was also funny and exciting. Billy was different. He was the biggest bully in the school, the nasty scare-you-to-death kind.

'There's this boy at school …' she began slowly. 'He's, he's …' she blinked away a hot tear. Suddenly, all her words shot out like exploding bullets. 'Billy's got goofy teeth and big fat red cheeks, and he throws crayons at me, and tips waste-paper baskets over my head and he sticks his foot out and hurts me!' Lily looked down at her left leg. This last bit was really painful. 'And he calls me 'Lily Black-boot' and 'Limpy-leg' and other things,' she finished in a barely-there voice.

Bast and Windy were silent for a moment.

Lowering her head, Bast said quietly and firmly. 'Lily, I want to apologise for my previous rudeness to you. I –'

'So you should!' Windy butted in. In a sing-song voice she chanted, 'Bast made a BIG mistake, Bast made a big mistake!'

'Life is not about making mistakes,' Bast said calmly. 'It's about what you do after you have made them. Now, let's see what we can do to help Lily, shall we?'

The expression on Windy's face quickly changed from wild-eyed to wistful. Darting up, she pulled out a tiny white hanky and dabbed it at the corner of Lily's eye. 'Please, don't cry. I'll be your friend if you want. And I can help you,' she added smiling.

Lily shook her head. 'No-one can help me,' she said sadly. 'But maybe I can help you, Windy. You must be lost. Maybe I can help you find your way home again?'

'My home is at the Angel of the North,' said Windy proudly. 'Do you know how to get there?'

'I think so.'

'Good. I have a zap.'

'A what?'

Windy's face flushed bright red. 'Oh. I mean map … I have a map,' she added quickly. 'Sometimes, when I get excited, I say the wrong thing and get my words muddled up.'

Lily looked at Windy with kindness in her eyes. Mummy was always telling her off for saying the wrong thing. 'It's okay, Windy,' she said softly.

'Okay? Okay?! Of course it's okay!' said Windy huffily. 'You be careful what you say to me, little girl. I might be a young fairy finding my way, but I'm super-duper clever, and don't you forget it!'

Reaching down deep inside her right boot, she pulled out a scroll of paper. It was covered in sparkling yellow dust. 'I had to leave the Angel of the North Fairy Academy,' Windy said matter-of-factly.

'For being an extremely naughty fairy!' hissed Bast.

Windy frowned. 'And Bast is my guardian,' she continued. She looked up at Lily. And for the very first time, Lily saw a tiny speck of fear in her eyes. 'Can you really help us find our way back home?'

Lily nodded. 'I think I can. I can try.'

Windy's eyes brightened. 'What a stroke of lovely luck! You can help us – and we can help you beat your bully, Billy Moonface. Brilliant! After all, one good turn deserves another – right?'

Lily nodded again.

'Good,' said Windy. 'Oooops! Just a minute, I've got an itch.' Poking her wand over her shoulder and down between her wings, she rubbed it up and down. The tip crackled and fizzed like a firework. 'Oh, shush, willy-wally plonkerwand! Ahhhhh … that's better. Now, where was I? Oh yes, I can help you, Lily. I can. We both can – can't we, Bast?'

Bast nodded her head approvingly. 'Windy, show Lily our map.'

Slowly, very slowly, Windy unrolled the sparkling golden scroll. Stroking it with her wand, she smoothed it out over the bed. Lily's eyes practically popped out of her head because when Windy had pulled it from her boot, the map had been small. Now, however, it stretched from her pillow right down to the foot of her bed. There were lots of funny drawings, and a long winding line that looked a lot like a train track, but

'WINDY, ARE THEY REAL EYES ON YOUR WINGS?' WHISPERED LILY.
'OR FUNNY BITS OF DUST?'

best of all, from top to bottom it sparkled like a magic golden carpet. Which, in actual fact, it was!

'Oh! It's beautiful!' Lily exclaimed, clapping her hands together.

'Why, thank you,' the map replied politely in a polished posh voice. 'And so are you!'

The voice had come from the end by the pillow, which had curled over into a gummy smiling mouth.

'You can talk?!' Lily squealed excitedly. 'Ooooh! Say something more!'

'Tally-ho! Tally-ho! Tally-ho-ho-ho!' the map sang out. 'Where would you like to go-go-go?'

Bast sighed loudly. 'Lily, we really haven't the time for this.'

'Oh … but I want to –'

'You can have your chat with the map another time,' Bast interrupted. She waggled a claw at a drawing near the map's mouth. 'That's the start of our journey. The fairies call it Father Christmas' rocket. Their magic stardust helps it fly. You will know it as Herd Groyne Lighthouse.'

Lily stared down at the sparkling map – and then the amazing golden dust twinkling between the tufts on the white carpet. It was the dust that had puffed out from Windy's boot. She looked at Windy. The same golden dust shimmered and sparkled all through her wings.

'Windy, are they real eyes on your wings?' whispered Lily. They were tiny, but they looked real. And the more Lily stared, the more they twinkled, winking at her. 'Or funny bits of dust?'

Instantly, the twinkling golden dust faded and every eye closed.

'I can't see the magic now,' Lily said, startled. 'Just the dust.'

'That's what a grown-up would say,' snarled Windy suspiciously. She stared into Lily's eyes. 'You're not a grown-up pretending to be a child, are you?' She fluttered over to Bast and whispered into her ear. 'It can happen, can't it? Demeanor the Witch's powers are getting stronger all the time.'

Bast sighed. 'The witch's powers are already stronger than yours.' She hung down her head. 'Soon, they will be stronger than mine.'

Lily gulped. *Witch! Did Bast say 'a witch?'* 'I can't help you,' she said in a panicky voice. 'I'm not brave enough, not like you and Bast. Mummy says a magpie pinched her real baby and put me in its place! So, you see, I can't come with you. I'm not brave and … and I'm not clever enough to see all the magic you see.'

'Listen carefully,' said Bast gently. 'Can you see the air that you breathe?'

Lily thought for a moment. She shook her head.

'There you are then. Just because you can't see something doesn't mean to say it's not there.

You might be cleverer – and braver than you think. What do you think Windy? Shall we take her?' The cat winked mischievously. 'Do you think Lily will be able to help us on our journey, or not?'

'Of course!' Windy said. 'We need your help, Lily. Stardust magic is as important to me as the air that you breathe. Without it, I can't fly. And if I can't fly, my wings will shrivel.' Her voice lowered to a whisper, 'I will die.'

'Oh!' Lily gasped. 'That's horrible! Please let me come. I can try and help – and Slobberchops, he must come too. He's the bestest dog in the whole world!'

'You mean that smelly old dog chewing on a bone downstairs?'

'He's not smelly! He's my bestest friend. Well, okay, maybe he smells a little bit.'

The cat wrinkled up her nose. 'A smelly dog flying on our magic carpet? I don't think so! So here is the Groyne,' Bast continued smoothly before Lily could say another word. She lifted her paw and patted the map in a circle. As Bast talked, Windy fluttered over and tiptoed along the line that looked like a train track. 'And here,' Bast added, dabbing at a drawing, 'is Father Christmas' rocket, standing at the mouth of the River Tyne at South Shields.'

Lily stared. It did look just like a big rocket about to blast off.

'And this,' Bast continued, running a claw just in front of Windy's feet, 'is the trail we need to follow to get to our home at the Angel of the North. Do you see? It runs right along the coastline from our first destination, Herd Groyne Lighthouse, and on to Souter Lighthouse. Then it winds along to the lighthouse at Parson's Rocks on the cliff edge, before swinging west along the River Wear towards Penshaw Monument. This is where the magic will take us – unless, of course, the witch gets there first ...'

The map was quite detailed. The more Bast talked, the more magical and amazing Lily thought the sea and the drawings and the lighthouses were. But she wished the map would talk again. Its mouth was open but funny gurgling noises kept popping out, as if it had gone to sleep and was dreaming. Lily bit her lip. She had forgotten all about Mummy. Now she could hear her slippers slip-slap-slopping along the corridor downstairs! Soon she would come up, she would have her shocked and angry face on – and her anger might make all the magic vanish. But the mysterious map was fascinating, and Lily just could not stop staring.

Leaning over, she traced her finger along the line. 'What's that?' she asked, jabbing her finger at a drawing of a long thin body with long arms outstretched wide. Of all the drawings on the map, Lily thought this was the strangest. 'Where's its nose? Why hasn't it got eyes or a mouth?' she asked, astonished.

'Perhaps the artist got bored and fell asleep?' giggled Windy.

Lily slapped her hand over her mouth, stifling a laugh.

Bast leapt up onto the windowsill, her fur bristling. 'It's a blank canvas to be written on,' she replied through gritted teeth. 'What is not fully understood should be treated with the highest respect. You and Lily both have a lot to learn.'

And then everyone fell silent as, deep in thought, six eyes glared down at the picture of the ridged brown body and blank featureless face. With the tip of her wand, Windy traced the outline from its fused-together toes, up the thigh and along one long flat wing, finishing at the top of its peculiar domed head.

'This,' Windy began, striking the forehead dead-centre, 'is the Angel of the North Fairy Academy. My home.'

Suddenly, from the bottom of the stairs, Mrs Bloom yelled: 'Lily! Put yourself to bed tonight. Mummy is busy.' In a screechier tone, she added, 'Have you seen that darn cat?'

The cat quickly put her paw over her lips.

'No, Mummy,' Lily fibbed. 'I haven't seen the cat.'

'Mind you don't let her in your bedroom. And clean your teeth properly!'

'Yes, Mummy.'

Bast smiled, and her whiskers twitched approvingly. 'I would like to thank you, Lily, for not telling your mummy I am in your room.'

'I don't like telling fibs,' said Lily. 'Was that naughty?'

'Well, maybe just a little bit naughty!' Bast replied, laughing. 'What you might call a white lie.'

'What's a white lie?'

'I had a feeling you were going to ask me that. It's like sweeties mixed with horrid-tasting medicine – a lot of good coming out of doing something strange and horrible. Understand?' Lily shook her head innocently. 'Well, never mind. You will when you're older. Anyway, Windy and I think you were kind – and,' she added, lowering her voice, 'brave.'

Windy darted up. Waving her wand and wiggling her bottom, she did a merry little jig in the air. 'Brave, brave, oh what a rave – Lily is brave!' she sang cheerily.

Lily blushed. A fuzzy warmth was growing inside her, like a tiny, stretchy hot water bottle slowly filling up.

'I'm not really,' she whispered. 'Windy,' she added with a little giggle. 'Can you show me some of your magic?'

Bast let out a low, growling purr.

'Delighted!' squealed Windy, turning her back on the cat. 'What would you like me to do?'

Lily thought of her three wishes; one had already come true. She had met a cheeky mischievous bat, a tiny feisty fairy, and a queen-like impossibly snooty cat. Perhaps now was the time for even bigger magic? Or maybe Windy could do a little spell to start with? Lily ran her tongue over her teeth. They felt okay, but Mummy would say they were dirty. She stared around her bedroom. Apart from the sprinkling of yellow fairy dust on the carpet, everything looked tidy clean and white – just the way Mummy liked it.

'Can you make my teeth so sparkling white even Mummy will say they are clean? No, wait – can you make my room messy, and … and, can you splish-splash everything in my bedroom with paint? Make it like a … like a … a crazy rainbow?'

'I can!' squealed Windy waving her wand over her head. 'But first: your teeth! Willy wallywand …' she sang, jiggling her bottom about merrily. 'Chilly dum-dum wumple dum-dum, clean teeth, clean teeth. Lily is going to have green teeth! Clean, I mean clean!' she added quickly.

But it was too late.

With a crackle and a fizz, the wand leaped out of Windy's hand. Seconds later, the glowing tip was poking out of Lily's mouth.

'Stop!' yelled Windy.

*Fzzzzzzzzzz*. The wand sprang out of Lily's mouth and dropped to the floor.

Dragging her left leg, Lily crawled over to the long mirror in the far corner of her bedroom. With two fingers, she pulled back the sides of her mouth and stared into the mirror. Windy's magic hadn't worked. Her teeth hadn't changed one little bit.

Looking down from the windowsill, the cat had been observing Lily struggle across the room. Now her tail shot up in a question mark.

'What's wrong with your leg?' she asked, astonished.

'It doesn't work. Well, it does a little bit.' Lily pointed at her leg brace propped up against the wall beside her bed. 'When I wear that.'

'Put it on,' said Windy. 'I want to see.'

'Be very careful, Windy …' hissed Bast. 'You aren't ready for big magic yet.'

Lily crawled back to her bed and hauled herself up. Balancing on the edge, she pulled on the brace and fastened the straps.

Windy fluttered over. 'Yuk!' she gasped, jabbing her wand at the thick black straps over Lily's leg. 'That looks holly-orry-orrid! Have no fear,' she added in a sing-song voice, 'Windy's here!'

'Nooooo!' screamed Bast. But it was too late.

'Big bad brace,' Windy chanted frantically, jabbing at it like a tiny sword-fighter, 'I don't like your face. Walk wild, high and true, chilly-bum-boo! Off. Off. Off with you!' The wand crackled. It was confused: Windy's spell was rubbish. Walk high?

**WHIZZ!** SUDDENLY LILY FOUND HERSELF HANGING UPSIDE DOWN FROM THE CEILING.

*Whizz!* Suddenly Lily found herself hanging upside down from the ceiling.

'No! No!' Windy screamed, dropping her wand. 'Walk, Lily! Walk your socks – I mean, walk your brace off!' That didn't make much sense to the wand either, but it did its best.

Seconds later, Lily did walk – sort of. Stiff-legged, squeaking, clunking and clacking like a rusty old robot, Lily marched all the way across the ceiling, down her bedroom door and across the floor. With a final clunk, she stopped in front of her mirror. Even before Lily saw her reflection, she knew the brace was still clamped on. It pinched her skin more than ever, like an extremely angry crab, and the straps felt like fat snakes, squeezing and sneaking round, nibbling and nipping, rubbing and pinching.

Windy dropped her wand. 'I'm sorry, Lily,' she said jumping up and stamping on the wand. 'It's this stupid wand's fault.' She jumped on it again.

'You are too young to use big magic wisely,' Bast scolded Windy. 'You young ones are always in a rush! You must learn to think before you act. Does Father Christmas deliver his presents without thinking first about where he is going? Of course not! Think. Plan. Act! That's the way to do it!' Fixing her eyes on Lily, she took a long deep breath, and then in a lilting, lively and strong voice, she began to sing:

*Lily walk strong, Lily walk true,*
*I believe in magic, I believe in you!*
*Your vision is wise and your heart*
*   is kind.*
*Now seek out your purpose and then*
*   you will find:*
*The greatest of magic is all in the mind!*

'There! See, Windy? That's how you do it! It's not complicated.'

'It is,' whined Windy. She crossed her arms and huffed. 'I didn't understand one single word of that spell.'

'That's because it was meant for Lily, not you. Look. See how my spell has made the brace lose its power?'

Everyone stared at Lily's bare leg. The brace had shifted. Now it lay obediently on its side by Lily's feet. 'Pick it up, Lily,' ordered Bast.

Legs wobbling, Lily did as she was told. Bast strode along the windowsill and opened the window. 'Now throw it out!' she commanded.

'But Mummy will be cross!'

Bast's eyes narrowed, and then she gave Lily such a fierce and menacing glare she couldn't possibly ignore her. With one big swing, Lily hurled the brace straight through the open window.

# CHAPTER FOUR

~~~~~~~~

*E*veryone stared out the window.

What have I done?! That was Lily's first thought. She had an almost overwhelming urge to run downstairs and pick it up before Mummy saw it. She giggled, nervously. But her next thought had her smiling. The ugly boot had whizzed out of the window – and vanished. That was shocking ... and wonderful!

'Now walk, Lily!' urged Bast. 'Walk like you walk in your dreams!'

Lily took a small hesitant step. Then another, then another.

'Oh!' she shrieked, jumping up and down. 'Oh! Oh! Oh!'

'Does it hurt?' asked Windy.

'Oh, no. It's magical. Look! I'm not limping!'

'Okay. That's enough *ohs*...' huffed Windy moodily.

'Windy, be pleased for Lily,' Bast said gently but firmly, 'and learn from this.'

Lily clapped her hands together. 'Thank you! Thank you! Thank you, Bast!' she exclaimed, laughing.

'Wishes do come true sometimes, don't they?!' Bast smiled – but Lily saw her eyes had a sad, distant look.

'They do! They do! Look!' Going up on tiptoe, Lily did a little twirl on the spot. 'See! I can move both legs. I can dance!'

'Okay, okay,' huffed Windy. 'So Bast's spell worked. Yippee for Bast and yippee for you!' She had her fingers crossed behind her back as she added: 'But maybe my first spell has worked now too? Let me see. Open your mouth, Lily. Open really wide.'

Lily stopped dancing. Leaning in towards the mirror, she opened her mouth.

'Oh!' she exclaimed. And then she giggled. Her teeth shone back at her like a row of tiny sparkling green emeralds. Magic! 'Do it! Do it again!' she shouted. 'Make my bedroom a horrible, disgusting mess! Make it blue, pink, red, green, yellow –'

'*Noooo!*' yelled Bast.

But Windy was already waving her wand again. Her success had made her even more reckless: 'Bedroom, by gum tidy and white,' she chanted, waving the wand around wildly. 'We don't care! Splish! Splash! Shake it all about. Willy wallywand, chilly bum-bum wumple dum-dum, splish splash your colour on walls and floors and everywhere!'

Instantly, like a sprung rubber band, the wand pinged out of Lily's hand and across her bedroom. Crackling and hissing, it whizzed to the ceiling, slid down the wall and swept over the bed before prancing and dancing its way over to the window. Bast pranced around the room too, hissing curses and taking wild swipes, but there was no stopping the magic wand now. Whizzing up onto the windowsill, it skated along the whole length before *tap tap tapping* its way up the windowpane. Jumping up, Bast took another wild swipe – and her claw clipped the wand! Hissing and spinning like a Catherine wheel, it shot across the room straight towards the door. There was a *bang!*, a soft *pop!*, and then with an exhausted gasp, the wand collapsed to the floor.

Everyone froze. Windy had done her best, the wand had done its best, but absolutely nothing in the room had changed.

*Poor Windy,* thought Lily, *she looks so sad.* 'Your wand is naughty,' she said, trying to be kind.

But Bast was shocked – and angry. 'You're a fairy who can't do magic,' she hissed. 'And a fairy without magic is about as much use as … as a smile with green teeth!'

Bast had hardly spat the words out before the magic began to happen. First, a mischievous wind blew in through the doorway and, to everyone's surprise and delight, as if from an invisible train, a black cloud puff-puff-puffed its way over the floor until the whole carpet was striped in thick bands of black and white. Lily giggled: her carpet looked just like a crazy zebra crossing! Even Bast thought it amusing, although, hiding her smile behind her paw, she tried not to show it. Next it was the wall's turn. Suddenly giant splodges of gaudy yellow covered all four walls, the curtains by the window and both sides of her bedroom door. And the magic didn't stop there. Just as Lily thought it couldn't get any more weird and amazing, a huge scarlet cloud of glittering red dust *whooshed* in through the doorway. Lily heard another longer *whooooosh* and, looking up, she saw the ceiling light had vanished. In its place hung an ominous black bag!

'Green and blue,' shrieked Windy in a frenzy, 'green and blue, we want you!' Instantly glowing like a red-hot poker, the magic wand whizzed up to the ceiling. The third jab did the trick.

*Bang!* Out flew thousands upon thousands of dancing blue and green bits and bobs, and teeny tiny twinkling spots.

'Some big, some small, some you can hardly see at all!' Windy sang merrily as the magnificent blue and green whirlwind swirled round and around Lily's bedroom.

'Oh!' she exclaimed, clapping her hands together. 'You did it. You did it!'

Windy stamped her boots triumphantly. 'See!' she squealed. 'Told you! Told you I could do it! I just need practice. Now, watch this. Wand, come here!' she commanded. Obediently the wand swooped down from the ceiling and popped itself onto Windy's open palm.

'Bumble wumble,' she chanted, 'everything tumble!'

Leaping up onto the windowsill *'Noooo!'* shrieked Bast.

Lily ran to her bed, kneeled on the edge and clapped her hands over her eyes. And she kept them there, even when she felt her bed shaking, her drawers sliding open, the swish of clothes tumbling out, hangers clanging, *plink plonk plink plonk* drums playing, teddies squeaking, dolls and toys and fluffy animals singing and swinging and jingling and …

Suddenly, everything stopped. Lily peeked through two fingers. Slobberchops was standing in the doorway looking gobsmacked. He was gawping at the yellow-splashed walls, the glittering scarlet dust, and the drawers and clothes and toys all piled up into a wobbling pyramid on the black and white carpet. It was a jumble-tumble, disgustingly awful mess. And in the middle of it all, perched on the windowsill licking her paw as if she couldn't give a tiddly-poo, sat the cat.

'The *cat!*' growled Slobberchops. This was all that darn snooty cat's doing! Stretching his neck, he let out a long ear-splitting: 'Y-I-K-E-S! Slobberchops to the rescue!' With a heroic leap, long ears spinning like windmills in a whirlwind, Slobberchops dashed across the room to save Lily from the dastardly doings of the bad white cat!

Flying quickly across the room, Windy thrust out her wand, right in front of the dog's face. 'Stop doggy!'

It was a mischievious and definitely dangerous thing to do. With a screechy 'H-e-l-p!' and sliding to a sudden halt, Slobberchops narrowly missed receiving a painful poke up the nose! Growling low, he swivelled his eyes sideways – and his jaw dropped with shock. The stick was being waved by a teeny-tiny creature … with wings!

Bast looked down from the windowsill, a look of total contempt on her face. 'Windy! Have you forgotten already? What did I tell you? Think. Plan. Act. Had you done so, you would have realised I am more than capable of looking after myself. That was a very foolish thing to do!' With a sniff she added: 'You might have hurt the soppy dog!'

'It's okay, Slobberchops,' said Lily kindly. She patted her bed. 'Come here.'

Head slung low, Slobberchops padded over to the side of Lily's bed. 'This is my friend, Windy,' she said pointing. 'She's a fairy and she's very, very clever and she can do really amazing magic and … Slobberchops! What are you doing? Come out from under my bed!'

'I'm going to get the blame for all this mess,' barked Slobberchops glumly. 'I know it. I just know it.'

'Oh, keep your stinky fur on,' giggled Windy. 'I can soon magic it all back to normal again.'

'But I don't want you to. Not yet, anyway,' pleaded Lily. 'I love it all messy and jumbled and upside-down.

It's … it's … wonderful! Make more magic Windy! Please! Make Slobberchops fly!'

'That's quite enough!' roared Bast. But then she added softly: 'Lily, you must understand something. I want you to look very carefully at Windy's wings.'

Lily stared at Windy's tiny beautiful wings. Every eye still winked, but along the tip of each wing, some eyes had faded. They looked cloudy, a sickly grey-green – and ghostly.

'Every time Windy or I do a spell, some of the magic dust vanishes and is gone forever. Now, take a look at her boots.'

Lily stared down at Windy's boots. They were flickering, like two light bulbs about to fizzle out.

'See how pale they are? That's because they are also losing their power. And her wand is weak too. The eyes, the wand and the boots are all warning us that there is very little magic stardust left.' Her voice lowered to a barely-there whisper. 'When all the stardust has gone, Windy will die – and so will I.' In a firm, clear voice she continued: 'Windy must practise to make her magic spells stronger – but she mustn't waste her stardust on tricks, or badly thought-through magic.'

A lump swelled up in Lily's throat. Bast's face was stiff and solemn. Windy looked sad – and alone.

'Windy –' began Lily.

'We must tell you why we are here, Lily, and not waste any more time,' Bast butted in. 'The truth is, Windy is dying.'

Lily gasped.

'This is where you can help us, Lily,' Bast continued quickly. 'The stardust Windy needs to save her life is the same magic dust we need to fly us all the way back to our home at the Angel of the North. It's hidden in secret chambers in lighthouses and ancient buildings, and Windy's map shows us exactly where those magical places are along the north-east coastline. Herd Groyne Lighthouse in South Shields is where our journey begins.'

'I can help!' Lily burst in excitedly. 'I know where the lighthouse is! It roars like an angry bear and makes a big loud noise to stop ships crashing into the pier. And it's right on the beach near the Little Haven Hotel.'

'This is a dangerous journey, Lily,' Bast continued solemnly. 'If you agree to go on our quest with us, you will enter our world: a world of fierce dragons and –'

'And Demeanor the Witch!' Windy burst in.

'Is she a real witch?'

'Oh, yes. If you agree to go on this adventure with us, you will step into another world where witches are very real. And Demeanor is the biggest, baddest, most evil witch of all. She has her spies everywhere. If Demeanor captures Windy, she will turn her into one of her slaves – she might even eat her!'

'Slaves!' Lily gasped.

'You must have seen them – on South Shields beach near the Little Haven Hotel. They look like a mysterious group of sculptures with pot bellies and no legs.'

'I have! I have seen them!' Mummy calls them the Weebles like my wobbly Weeble toy. I tried to push one over but it wouldn't move. Are they deaded?'

'You mean dead?'

Lily nodded.

'Oh much worse than dead Lily! Demeanor's slaves are known as Dark Fairies – sad creatures who cannot hear, move or speak. But on the night of a full moon, the witch gives them back their wings and legs. Then she makes them do cruel wicked things. Demeanor is the Queen of Witches and will capture and destroy anyone who gets in her way. And that means you too, Lily. You could get trapped in our world, you could even die, and then in your world it will be as if you have gone to sleep and cannot wake up. Think carefully before you give us your answer, Lily. Do you still want to go on this journey?'

Lily shivered. It was really happening. Her second and her third wish were coming true. But was this really what she wanted? What if she wasn't brave enough to fight a witch? What if the evil witch captured her and turned her into one of her slaves?

The words the wise cat said next Lily did not fully understand, but would always remember: 'Feel the fear, and do it anyway. Fear has many faces,' she added sagely. 'When we leap into the unknown, one vanishes – and every other face turns, and winks.' And then the cat winked.

'Come with us!' urged Windy. 'Go on, Lily. Take a leap into the unknown!'

'If you never leap, you will never know,' added Bast.

And then Lily knew what she must do. She smiled at Bast. And as the cat smiled back, her long whiskers flickered with pride and her tail shot up like a flagpole. 'This will take BIG magic,' Bast said earnestly, 'from someone whose powers already equal Demeanor's. Do you know anyone like that, Lily?'

Lily shook her head.

'Are you sure?'

She shook her head again.

'Oh, I think you do. Does the name Benjamin-bat ring a bell?'

Later that same night, lying in bed and cuddling up to Slobberchops, Lily snuggled her face into his. His fur felt soft and warm. Lifting his fluffy ear-flap, she whispered: 'It all makes sense now, doesn't it?'

Like most things, it didn't make any sense at all to Slobberchops, but it seemed important to Lily that it did, so he nodded his head enthusiastically.

'Don't you see? I made three wishes. Benji-bat heard them and now they are coming true. We're going to fly, Slobberchops. Soon we're going to fly!'

Lily felt her eyelids getting heavy. Bast and Windy's last words still rang in her ears like the biggest, noisiest bell in the world.

'First we'll get Benjamin-bat's help,' Bast had announced.

'We fly to the Groyne Lighthouse tomorrow night,' Windy had added excitedly. 'It's a full moon, and my energy will be at its strongest. But tomorrow is your day, Lily, the day you face your demons – and Billy Moonface!'

'But what spell will you do?' Lily had asked. 'Demeanor is the biggest bully in your world, but Billy Moonface is the biggest and baddest in mine!'

'Wait and see!' Windy had replied, somewhat unhelpfully.

Lily shut her eyes, and that very same moment, just behind her eyelids, Billy's grinning face exploded into view. She trembled. And then a sudden, terrifying thought spun out of nowhere and erupted inside her head.

*What if witches can see inside you? What if they can see you're not brave?*

'Feel the fear, and do it anyway,' she whispered to Slobberchops.

Slobberchops sat up quickly on the bed. 'What fear?' he asked astonished. 'Don't worry Lily. Whatever it is, I will protect you!'

Lily tugged at one of the dog's fluffy ears. 'Silly Slobberchops. Get back into bed!'

'I'm a guard,' Slobberchops said proudly. 'I'm guarding you!'

'Quick then. There's something furry crawling around by my feet!'

Diving under the covers and burrowing down the bed, the dog snuffled around Lily's feet. Finally, 'Where?' he yelped confused. 'There's nothing here!'

'Oh yes there is,' Lily giggled. 'You are!'

'Harumph!' Slobberchops sighed. He licked Lily's wiggling toes, and then rested his head between her feet.

'I love you Slobberchops,' Lily said sweetly. With her big toe she tickled along his nuzzle. 'You're not the smartest dog in the world, but you are loving. And loving is much much better than being smart. Now be a good dog and go to sleep.'

Immediately, and as if by magic, their eyes closed, and they both fell fast asleep.

Next morning when the loud rumbling of the hoover woke her up, Lily opened her eyes and stared around. Everything in her bedroom was back in its place – clean and tidy – with one new addition. On the shelf by the mirror, nestling amongst her teddies, sat Windy, also all in white. Lily stared. Snuggled in next to Lily, Slobberchops stared too. Windy looked stiff, frozen and lifeless, like a china doll.

'Hide, Windy!' Lily shouted. But it was too late. Mrs Bloom, her hoover and her feather duster were already grumbling, rumbling and feathering their way up the stairs, and into her bedroom.

'How do you get so much dirt in your bedroom, Lily?' Mrs Bloom groaned. 'I don't know. Why have I got such an untidy girl for a daughter?'

Lily sat bolt upright. Perhaps Mummy would think Windy was a doll. But what if Windy moved?

But Windy didn't move – not even when Mrs Bloom wiped her feather duster right across Windy's face, tickling her frozen nose! Lily slipped back under her duvet and pulled it over her head. Slobberchops slid back under the covers too and dived to the bottom of the bed.

MRS BLOOM SWIPED HER FEATHER DUSTER RIGHT ACROSS WINDY'S
FACE, TICKLING HER FROZEN NOSE!

# CHAPTER FIVE

~~~~~~~~~~~~~~~~~~~~~~~~

'**H**urry up, lazy-bones, get your leg brace on and get started. I can't be wasting time.' At the doorway, Mrs Bloom turned. She stared up at the shelf.

'That's very odd …' she muttered. 'I don't remember buying you a china doll.'

Lily wanted the bed to swallow her up. What if her mother grabbed hold of Windy?

'Hurry up, girl,' said Mrs Bloom sharply. 'Don't just lie there. You'll be late for school.' And then with a loud 'Tut!', she turned and waddled out of the bedroom. Lily popped her head out from under the duvet, just in time to see her wardrobe door swing wide open. Bast strolled out, yawning widely.

'Oh, Bast, quick! Look! Windy's not moving!'

'It's her spell,' said Bast wearily. 'She wanted to see if she could turn herself into a china doll!'

Lily jumped out of bed. Without thinking about what she was doing, she ran over to the shelf by the door. 'Oh!' she cried, looking down at her legs. 'I can run!'

'Of course you can, Lily!' Bast said cheerily. 'But only when we are around.'

'Then I must be dreaming.' She stared around her pristine, tidy room, then back at Bast. 'But if I'm dreaming, then you're not real, are you?'

Bast's fur bristled and her tail shot up. 'What nonsense!' she hissed. 'Lily, I'm surprised at you! I'm as real as real can be!' She shook her head and sighed. 'But Windy …' she added without finishing her sentence.

'Is she deaded?' Lily whispered.

Bast lifted her paw and licked it slowly. 'I really wouldn't know.'

'But why doesn't she move?' Reaching up, she grabbed hold of Windy's leg and dragged her off the shelf. 'Move!' she pleaded, giving her a good shake. 'Are you deaded?' she whispered. Holding her close, she stared into Windy's eyes. They were wide open, unblinking. 'Wake up, Windy. Oh! Please, wake up. Bast, make her wake up. What did she do? Bast, what spell did she do?'

'If you must know,' Bast hissed through gritted teeth, 'Windy sang: *Chillydumdum make me still, make me white. Chillydumdi-dum, it will be all right, on the night!* I've never heard such a ridiculous spell in all my life!' She strolled over to the shelf, and stared up at Windy. 'Now she's like one of Demeanor's dark fairy slaves at the Groyne. Trapped inside, she can't speak and she can't move.' She sat down huffily. 'And it serves her right!'

'Please don't be cross with Windy. Look …' Lily gave the fairy another hard shake. 'Look, Slobberchops.' The dog popped his head out from under the covers. 'Windy might be deaded!'

'You mean dead,' said Bast matter-of-factly.

'Yes – deaded! Oh, pleeease help her, Bast!'

'Windy must take her spells more seriously. She has a lot of growing up to do. All this chilly dumdi-dum business …' Her tail whipped back and forth uppishly and angrily. 'It's so undignified! She must wake up and smell the coffee, or she's going to get us into a lot of hot water!'

Lily was about to ask what the smell of coffee had to do with anything when, suddenly, Windy leaped straight out of her hands.

'Fooled you!' she squealed, darting around the room.

'Windy! You're not deaded!' squealed Lily.

'Awesome!' yelped Slobberchops.

'That was close! Wow, Lily. Your mum's a bit of a weirdo, isn't she?'

'She likes everything to be perfect,' said Lily quietly. 'And I'm not.'

'Well that makes two of us!' giggled Windy. 'Now, it's off to school with you. Billy Moonface is waiting.'

Lily felt panic rising in her throat. 'But aren't you coming with me?'

Windy shook her head.

'Bast, will you come with me?'

'My place is beside Windy.'

Lily bit her lip. She bit so hard she could feel a strange sour taste in her mouth. How could they stop Billy Moonface bullying her if they weren't even there?

Bast looked suddenly grave. 'Aren't you forgetting something, Windy?'

Windy shrugged her shoulders.

'Sit down,' Bast said sharply. 'I can't talk to you properly when you're fluttering about like a fairy.'

'But I am a fairy!' She swooped down in a sulk, perched on the end of Lily's bed and kicked out her legs. 'That's what young fairies do. They kick and flutter and fly. And anyway, I've got itchy wings. You'd flutter about too if you had itchy wings like mine.'

'That's enough of your cheek,' snapped Bast. 'Now listen carefully, both of you. Windy, you need to stop playing about with your spells and take this all much more seriously. That's what got you thrown out of Fairy Academy in the first place – or had you forgotten?'

Windy crossed her arms. 'I guess so,' she said grumpily.

'If you don't stop playing around with magic and wasting precious fairy dust, we will never find our way back to the Angel of the North.'

'Okay, okay,' said Windy. 'But you're no fun anymore, Bast. Weren't you ever young?'

'No,' she said, stretching her neck and poking her nose in the air. 'As a matter of fact, I wasn't.' She turned to face Lily. 'For Windy's spell to work with Billy Moonface, you must do something that at first you will find bizarre and mystifying. But it is vital that you persevere and do exactly what I ask of you with a good and open heart. Do you understand, Lily?'

Lily shook her head.

'Then I will explain. The universe is very generous with its gifts. And the gift of life is the most generous of all, of course. But we should never expect something for nothing. That's not the way to learn. For this magic spell to work, Lily, you must think of Billy in a very different way. Whenever you find yourself thinking about him, you must try to create good, positive thoughts and energy.'

Slobberchops' eyes glazed over. Lily screwed up her face – too many big words they both didn't understand.

'Tell me, Lily,' Bast said patiently, 'what do you think of Billy right now?'

'Well, he's fat and he's got these little piggy eyes and –'

'Stop! Stop! That's not what I meant. Imagine Billy Moonface is standing in front of you right now … What's going through your mind?'

Lily pursed her lips, desperately trying not to cry.

'Go on Lily,' Bast coaxed gently.

'I want to punch him on the nose. I want him to go away. I want him to fall down a big hole and never come back.'

'So, you want something really horrible to happen to him?' Lily nodded. 'And you want something horrible to happen to him because he does horrible things to you?' She nodded again. Bast stroked her chin thoughtfully for a few moments. Then, the cat smiled wryly.

'Very well. Then this is what you must do. From this moment on, every time you think of Billy Moonface, you must think nice thoughts. You must imagine him smiling at you as if he really likes you, and you must smile right back at him and mean it. Do you think you can do that?'

Lily frowned. How do you be nice to someone who is horrible? 'I don't know,' she answered truthfully. 'But I can try. Can't you come with me, you and Windy? I'll be okay if you are with me.'

'No, Lily, it's important that you do most of this on your own. Besides, Windy and I haven't eaten for days. She needs to stay right here and magic up some food for us.'

'And toffee!' Windy piped up. 'Caramel toffee is Bast's favourite sweet.'

'But cats don't eat sweets,' giggled Lily.

The cat walked around in a circle, head held high. 'I am not your common house cat,' she purred arrogantly. 'I am a superior being. It's allowed.'

'Mummy's got some chicken downstairs. I could creep into the kitchen fridge and get it for you.'

Hearing the word 'chicken', Slobberchops licked his lips. He was thinking, *Food, glorious food. Yum!* But the cat was insulted.

'That disgusting mush your mother stuck in a bowl by the door for me? Tsk! Absolutely not!'

'But you're a cat,' said Lily, astonished. 'Cats love chicken!'

'I told you, I am a superior being. And superior beings require superior food – and sweets.'

'Oh!' exclaimed Lily, wondering if 'superior being' meant alien. 'Then what do you eat?'

'Chocolate and pilchards. Lots of it – all mashed up together with caramel toffee and lashings of cream. Yummy.'

Lily had a sudden horrid taste in her mouth. 'Ugh!' she exclaimed. 'Chocolate, caramel and pilchards? That's icky-yukky! I couldn't do that.'

'That's why we have to stay here and Windy will magic it up for me. By the way, what do you like to eat, Lily?'

'Well, I like sweets, jelly babies and chocolate biscuits.'

'All together?'

'Ugh!' Lily gasped again. 'Nooooo!'

'I see – I think. And Slobberchops? What is his favourite food?'

'Dog food in a can.'

'Disgusting!' snapped Bast. 'No wonder he smells like dirty old socks. He can have a sausage and like it. Are you making a note of all this, Windy? We are all going to need packed lunches for our journey to Father Christmas' rocket at the Groyne. And while Lily's at school, you will be practising some **proper** magic.'

School! Now Lily felt desperate. Rolling her eyes, she put on her best little-girl-lost look. 'Can't I go on your journey with you first?'

'No, Lily. That's not the way the universe works. For you to step into our world, you must face your biggest demon first, or you will bring it with you. And your demon is *Billy Moonface*.'

'But I *want* you to come with me. You said I wouldn't be on my own. You promised. I need you!' she said desperately.

'We will be with you,' replied Bast gently. 'Just not in the way that you think. Oh, and watch out for the gremlin.'

'What's a gremlin?'

'A small, ugly creature with big ears, a long hot-rod tongue and a filthy temper. Watch out, Lily! Because very soon you're going to see more than one!'

Later that same morning, hobbling along on the road to school, Lily kept glancing back. Windy and Bast had to come, they had promised – sort of. Bast had said: '*We will be with you. Just not in the way that you think.*' That was a promise, wasn't it?

But the closer Lily got to the school gates, the more she panicked. Maybe it was all a trick? Windy and Bast had got Slobberchops into big trouble. When Mrs Bloom had found the leg brace lying on the front garden that morning, her cheeks had blown out like hot red balloons. She was really angry, and before Lily could say anything Slobberchops had got a big smack. There was nothing special about fairies – or their snooty guardian cats – Lily decided. They might have a bit of funny magic, but it was just silly tricks that went wrong, wrong, wrong.

Suddenly, the rusty iron school gates loomed large. 'Bye, Mummy,' Lily said, letting go of her hand. She hobbled across the playground, down the corridor and into her classroom. Her demon was sitting cross-legged on the mat next to her teacher, Miss James. Lily sat down at the back, as far away from Billy Moonface as she could get.

'Lily Bloom!' Miss James called out. 'You are late! The register has already been taken. Go to Mrs Snodgrass' office and tell her you are here, or you won't get your school dinner. Billy, you go with her.'

Billy couldn't believe his luck. Snooty Mrs Snodgrass' office was right down the end of the corridor. Plenty of time to beat Lily up – and no-one would see!

'Yes, Miss James,' he said, jumping up.

'That's a good boy, Billy. I'm giving you another chance to show you can behave yourself, so make sure you do.'

Lily opened her mouth to scream. No! No! No! Whenever Lily was scared though, no matter how hard or loud or long she screamed, nothing came out of her mouth. It was just as if her tongue suddenly had a huge gobstopper sitting on it.

Lily shuffled towards the door.

As soon as they were outside the classroom, Billy pushed his plump chest up against hers and shoved her against the wall. No one could help her now. Billy would kick and kick and kick at her leg brace until she fell down. Her fate was sealed. Or was it? The mysterious cat had told her that for nice things to happen, she must think nice thoughts.

Billy's grinning face was so close to Lily now, his disgusting, hurricane breath smacked against her cheeks and sizzled up her nostrils.

Suddenly, he punched his fist into the palm of his hand, right in front of her face. Before Lily could run, he had pinned her against the wall with his fists placed firmly either side of her shoulders. A shot of hot panic ran through Lily's body. She just could not stop trembling. But for the first time, Lily saw something that she had never seen before – and it was the last thing in the world she expected to see in Billy's watery blue eyes: fear! Behind all the wild, angry bluster, Billy was scared! She smiled up at him. *Scared Billy, be nice to me. You can be nice if you try, Billy – you can, you can …*

Instantly and with little effort, Lily slipped out from under his arm.

Shuffling down the corridor with Lily leading the way now, Billy knew something weird and horrid had just happened – he just didn't know what. *Still*, he thought, looking down the empty corridor, *something's going right – everyone's in class.*

'Gotcha!' he sneered, running up quickly and kicking out his left foot. It should have sent Lily flying – that's what usually happened – but this time, his foot jerked and jittered. To Billy's mounting horror, it began spinning round faster and faster on the end of his leg. Scrunching up his toes, he tried kicking it out again. *Crack!* His lower leg bent the wrong way. Then his whole leg boomeranged right back up at him. It would be difficult to say who was more shocked as, with a loud *thump!*, Billy kicked his own chin!

Lily didn't know whether to laugh or cry. Rubbing his chin, Billy stared down at the rogue foot.

'Are you all right?' Lily asked sweetly. 'Your chin's very red.'

In his head, Billy was shouting 'Shut up!' – and that's what should have shot out of his mouth too. Only it didn't. Instead, in melodic lilting tones, out came: 'Sugar-plum! I love you, Lily Sugar-plum!'

'Huh?!'

'You are so sweet.' He clapped his hand over his mouth, spluttering the rest through his nail-bitten fingers. 'I l-l-l-love you, Lily!' And then he froze. This could not be happening! A zillion thoughts buzzed around in Billy's brain, like a bee with its bottom on fire. *Zzzip!* Zip! Zip! What the gazumping-zillio just happened? *Zzzip!* Zip! Zip!

Lily took a small step back, then another, then another. Until, suddenly, she was pounding down the corridor towards the office as fast as the brace clamped onto her leg would let her. Billy was running too – as fast as his thick, stumpy legs would let him.

The office door swung open. Mrs Snodgrass was behind her desk. She fixed her eyes on Lily, and then her thin, mean-looking mouth snapped: 'You late birds are a nuisance!' She shoved a big red book across the desk. 'Sign your name in the Late Book.' Stepping forward, Lily signed her name. 'A nuisance!' Mrs Snodgrass snapped again, slapping a huge yellow sticker on Lily's jumper.

'Haw haw!' sniggered Billy. 'Late bird, late bird!'

Lily stared at the sticker on her shoulder: a sad-eyed, long-necked chicken was kissing a bubble. Inside were some words.

'It says: "I am a naughty late-bird!" ' huffed Mrs Snodgrass. 'That's you, Lily Bloom!' Lily sucked in her breath, desperately trying to hold back her tears.

It worked – almost: one stinging hot droplet popped out from her left eye. Lily rubbed it away quickly.

'Cry-baby Bloom,' mouthed Billy.

'And what are you doing here, Billy?'

He shrugged his shoulders.

'Both of you back to class. Now! I've work to do.'

All the way back down the corridor to the classroom, Lily sang quietly: 'Fippity-fuppity foo, fippity-fuppity you! Fippity-fuppity foo, nasty Billy Moonface, I hate you!'

Twice, Billy swung round, a look of dark thunder on his face. And, twice, Lily ducked. But Billy was still feeling odd and his thoughts were not connecting properly. Instead of thumping her, he just mouthed silently, 'Shut up, or I'll bop you one!' Then he swung his arms about a bit, which Lily thought a little bit scary – and definitely very funny. Miss James was down the end of the corridor asking Amy loudly why she had pushed a pencil rubber up her nose.

When they reached the classroom, Lily was feeling less jumpy. Slipping alongside Billy, she glanced up. His cheeks were puffed out like cannonballs, and his blue eyes (now marbled with spidery red veins) glared back down at her menacingly. Even so, behind the mask, Lily could still see Billy's fear.

*Billy is nice, Billy is nice*, she chanted. She had no idea what she was doing, really, but to her surprise and delight, just thinking something nice instead of something horrible made her feel better – a little. *Billy is nice*, she chanted frantically in her mind. *He's scared, so he does nasty things. Nice Billy.* Glancing up, she thought: *But he looks horrible!* Trembling, taking deeper and deeper breaths, she continued chanting *Nice Billy – he's not all bad. Billy's just scared, scared scared.*

And then she said something out loud she had never even dared to think before, let alone say.

Standing up tall, in a cool strong voice she said: 'You're scared, Billy Moonface. That's why you bully! But I'm not scared of you! You are a stupid, stupid, stupid boy!' she added, in a slightly less than calm voice. Then she ducked!

To everyone's surprise (though mostly Billy's), he replied, 'Ah! Look at Lily. Isn't she wonderful!'

A deathly silence fell across the classroom. Billy gulped. That was just about the worst thing he could have done. Right up to that moment, the gremlin hiding inside his mouth (brought to life by Windy's spell) had been thoroughly enjoying himself, splashing about in a bubble bath of spit. Now it slithered superfast down Billy's throat – straight towards the gassy pile bubbling around in his stomach. The gremlin wasn't in the least bit worried. It simply stuck out its tongue, which just happened to be as hot as a sizzling red-hot poker!

Poke! Poke! Poke!

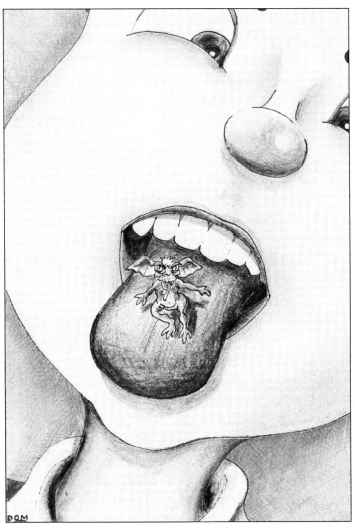

BILLY GULPED. THAT WAS JUST ABOUT THE WORST THING HE COULD
HAVE DONE.

Instantly, Billy's tongue whizzed around in his mouth like a sausage in a whirlwind. 'Aaaaaagh! I love you! I love you, Lily!'

It was at this precise moment when, dragging Amy behind her, Miss James walked back into the classroom. The door open, everyone had heard Billy yell he loved Lily – and everyone, including Lily, was laughing loudly. Amy was guffawing so much she gagged, and the pencil rubber shot out of her nostril like a bullet.

Meanwhile, Billy's cannonball cheeks were going from red to scarlet to a deep purple-blue. As Lily continued to watch open-mouthed, he began rocking– forwards, backwards, forwards, backwards.

Lily took a huge step back. She thought Billy might explode or faint, or maybe faint then explode, she wasn't sure which.

Miss James rushed over, looking shocked and worried. 'Billy? Are you all right, Billy?'

He didn't dare say 'No, Miss James' just in case something awful came out instead. Clapping his hands over his mouth, he shook his head.

'Go and sit back on the mat, Billy – away from Lily.'

Fortunately for everyone, the rest of the day went smoothly. Several times Lily took a sneaky look over at Billy, and every time he had his fingers down his throat desperately trying to yank something out.

At home time, Lily stood in a corner of the playground biting her bottom lip. Mummy was late picking her up. She looked around. Billy was by the school gate, kicking grit. And then suddenly his stumpy legs were bounding across the playground and he was there, in front of her, jamming his pudgy nose up against hers.

'What's wrong, Lily?' he asked in a cheerful and caring voice. He bit his tongue. It was happening again! All his words had come out okay this time, but instead of sounding nasty, his voice had sounded all soppy and mushy, as if he really cared! Had Lily cast a spell on him? Scratching his head, he snarled, 'I'll show you! Take this!' He lifted his right foot, as if to lash out at Lily, but then his leg suddenly decided not to bother and dropped back down again.

'Kick!' screamed Billy. 'Kick Lily!' But the foot wasn't listening.

'Piddle off!' it squeaked back.

Billy's jaw dropped to the floor and he did a sort of open-mouthed gulp. That was, in fact, another big mistake, because it was just enough time for another gremlin to jump inside his mouth, grab hold of his teeth and clamp them together! That's what gremlins do – the unexpected. And this one was no exception. This particular gremlin, however, was also in a mischievous mood, determined to have some fun. Grabbing hold of Billy's tongue, he twisted it round and round like a corkscrew, jumbling and tumbling up all Billy's spit until two foamy trails spurted out and down the sides of his mouth. Now Billy not only felt odd, he also looked odd: like a mad dog frothing at the mouth. Suddenly all the tumbling stopped. After a moment's silence while Billy panicked inwardly, he blurted out: 'I want to kiss you! I love you, Lily. You are wonderful and kind and you are sooooo pretty!'

The terrified look on Billy's face had to be seen to be believed, but like lava from an exploding volcano, the words just kept on spitting out. 'And you have lovely dark hair – and I like your sweet, pretty smile.' All kinds of wicked thoughts and words raced through Billy's mind, but the nice words kept on shooting out. And the more Billy tried to say nasty things to Lily, the nicer they came out! 'And you smell sweet, and I love you, love you, love you …'

Lily thought it couldn't get any more weird or amazing or funny until, finally, falling down on one knee and grabbing hold of her hand, Billy blurted out:

'Lily Bloom, will you marry me?!'

That night, as soon as Lily got home from school, she hobbled up the stairs as quickly as she could to her bedroom. Bast was up on the windowsill, staring out of the window and purring loudly.

'It worked!' Lily exclaimed. 'Your spell worked!' She slumped down on her bed. 'Oh, thank you, Bast and Windy. It worked, it worked!' she repeated, unstrapping her leg brace.

'Of course it did!' squealed Windy. She flew over from the shelf to the windowsill and, fluttering in the air alongside Bast, did a little curtsy.

Lily giggled. Pulling off her boot, she said, 'But Billy doesn't *really* love me, does he?'

'Goodness me, no!' exclaimed Bast. 'Magic can make people behave in certain weird and wonderful ways, but you can't *make* anyone love you for real. Billy has to be careful, though,' she added, chuckling. 'You see, Lily, if you say something often enough, you will start to believe it is true. That's why you should never call yourself bad names, or tell yourself you are daft or silly just because you make a mistake or can't do something. It's not true. But say it often enough and you may start to believe that it is.'

Windy fluttered in a circle around Bast's head. 'When I wake up in the morning,' she said, blonde curls bouncing merrily as she danced through the air, 'I tell myself I am a magical, wonderful being, full of light and love. And I am!'

Lily giggled again. She leaned the leg brace up against the wall under the window. Wiggling her toes, she leaned back, and kicking out both legs, she cycled them through the air like an upside down cyclist. It felt … amazing! But a quick glance over at her leg brace left her wondering, how long would this wonderful magic work?

The cat's green eyes glowed with pride as she said, 'You see, Lily, you stood up to Billy Moonface, you showed you had courage. That's what really made it all happen for you. Believe in yourself. I mean reeeally believe. We all live in a wonderful, magical universe where dreams can and do come true. But first you must believe – in the magic of … *you!*'

# CHAPTER SIX

'Give it a good swing, Lily', Bast said waggling her paw at the leg brace. 'And hurry up. We've no time to waste.'

Jumping off the bed, Lily grabbed hold of her leg brace. Raising it high over her head, she pointed it, boot end first, towards the open window. The straps were undone and they hung down, curling around her arms like long, fat rats' tails.

'Out you go, ugly boot!' Lily yelled. It was a really strong throw. And it was just as if the brace had grown wings, because the boot and its flailing straps flew out of Lily's bedroom window and vanished into the darkness.

Bast and Windy clapped and cheered. Slobberchops cheered too, in his delightful doggie way, running around in circles, yelping and chasing his tail.

'Well done, Lily!' Bast purred proudly. Licking her paw slowly, she smoothed out two of her long whiskers. 'Windy and I are very proud of you.'

Lily felt that same warm, fuzzy glow inside her she had felt once before. 'I wish I could jump like this all the time,' she said, jumping up and down on the spot.

Bast was purring so loudly now, Lily thought it sounded just like the engine of an ice-cream van.

'You have a beautiful mind and you have imagination,' the cat said smiling. 'As long as you believe you have that, Lily, the universe, with all of its magic and wonders, is yours.'

Five long minutes later, Bast was still sitting on the windowsill, only now she was hissing and her long tail lashed impatiently. Windy had been waving her wand about, chanting her spell – or trying to. 'Your spell is codswallop!' hissed Bast. And it was: the map was refusing to move.

'Harumph!' Slobberchops sighed loudly. *Bast is a bossy-boots. If she spoke like that to Lily, I'd bite her whiskers off!*

Perched carefully on the edge of her bed, trying not to crumple up the map, Lily's eyes followed the squiggly trail connecting the drawings. She shivered. There it was! Herd Groyne Lighthouse. Painted bright red and standing on twelve iron legs, it might look like a jolly Father Christmas rocket, but it held big, bad memories for Lily. A balcony ran round near the top of the lighthouse, and on a school trip, Billy had grabbed and swung her out over the edge, holding her by her leg brace. The leg brace had slipped, Miss James had screamed and Lily had almost hurtled head first to the ground!

The line ran along the coastline to Souter Lighthouse, which was painted in thick bands of red and white, and then on to the white-painted lighthouse at Parson's Rocks. *Demeanor could be hiding inside any one of those places*, she thought, biting her lip. *Perhaps in the chamber itself, where the stardust is hidden. And the witch has big, bad magic, perhaps a thousand times stronger than Windy's.*

The plan, Windy had said, was to snatch a little stardust from the chamber inside each lighthouse until there was just enough to fly them safely back to their home at the Angel of the North. Lily felt a little fluttering inside her chest where her heart was: two magical days had past since she had made her three wishes to Benji-bat. Now whenever Bast and Windy were around, she could walk, skip, run and play just like anyone else. Billy Moonface was being nice to her, she had the special new friends she had asked for, and now she was going on a mysterious and dangerous adventure!

A peculiar rustling noise burst into Lily's thoughts. Making little kittenish miaowing noises, the map was lifting, arching at the far end a little, straightening out and then arching back up again, slightly higher than before – like a cat shaking its bottom just before pouncing. Bast and Windy were arguing, and Windy had started shouting: 'I did not say like a *cat* on springs, I said **shake like a *map* on springs!**'

'No, no. You definitely said cat,' hissed Bast. 'My superior cat's ears distinctly heard you. Don't get so excited when you do your spells, Windy. Keep yourself serene and calm – like me.'

Taking a deep breath, Windy waved her wand. But before she could say anything, in a low earthy voice, Bast began to sing:

*A finer map I have never seen,*
*You are the one to live our dream,*
*Not a map with springs, but a map*
*  with wings,*
*Our journey's not over until the fat*
*  lady sings!*

Instantly, as if being smoothed over by a giant iron, the map straightened itself out. Rising up a few centimetres, it slid off the bed, hovered over to the middle of the room, and dropped to the floor.

Windy lowered her wand. '"Fat lady sings?" What fat lady? That's not a nice thing to say.'

'Well, it's just an old saying,' replied Bast, yawning widely. 'You wouldn't understand.'

'Huh?! Anyway – map's ready,' said Windy, fluttering her wings. 'Are you ready, Lily?'

Lily skipped across the room and jumped onto the map.

'Sit on Father Christmas' rocket,' commanded Bast. Hopping along the trail, Lily stopped at the drawing of the rocket. Toes tingling with nervous excitement, she tiptoed her way along the balcony.

'Okay – good,' said Windy, pointing her wand at the base of the rocket. 'Now, sit down.'

Lily sat down quickly and crossed her legs. Wagging his tail, Slobberchops padded over to the map and sat down in front of her. Windy pointed her wand again.

'Don't point your wand at me!' snapped Bast. 'And remember, none of your wumple-dum-dum codswallop. Do a proper spell.' Leaping down from the windowsill, she curled herself in behind Lily. 'We simply can't afford to waste any more stardust. Jump off, Slobberchops. You can wait here until Lily returns.'

What?! Lily rarely got angry, but this was so unfair! 'No! If Slobberchops can't come,' she shouted, 'I'm not going!' This promised to be the most amazing, scary and exciting of all journeys. 'Slobberchops **is** coming!' she added indignantly, crossing her arms.

'We're wasting time,' snapped Bast. 'Oh, all right – let the old dog come. But you must keep him quiet. One bark at the wrong time …' she hissed at Slobberchops, '… and you're dogs' meat!'

Slobberchops twisted around to face Lily. The astonished look on his face said: *Yikes! Now what have I done?*

Finally, sitting one behind the other on the map, Bast, Lily, Slobberchops and Windy were ready – almost.

'Okay,' Windy said impatiently. 'We' re all set to go now, aren't we?'

Bast stared at Windy, at her pale dull wings. 'Not quite.' And cupping her paws to her mouth, she yelled: 'B-E-N-J-A-M-I-N -B-A-T!'

Instantly 'Twit-twoo!' hooted cheerily above their heads. 'Just give your local Benjamin-bat a call! Benji-bat, at your service. And what can I do for you this starry, starry night?'

Stretching their necks, everyone looked up. The bat was hanging upside down from the ceiling light, swinging to-and-fro.

'We are on a dangerous quest,' Bast began solemnly. 'We must find more stardust, and soon, or Windy will die.' She took a deep breath. 'But Demeanor will be waiting for us.'

'The witch!' exclaimed Benjamin-bat. Swinging quickly round, he sat upright. Lily didn't like the look in his eyes. They were saucer-wide. A white ring circled each pupil, making him look scared – and scary.

'If I'm right, and I am because I'm always right, to fight a big, bad witch like Demeanor you will each need very special gifts, besides those you already have. Lily!' Benjamin-bat said, suddenly cheery.

'So very nice to see you again so soon. Stand up, little girl, and receive your gift from me.' Lily stood up. 'Now hold out your hands, palms upwards.' The bat lifted one wing and instantly something small and shiny spun out and tumbled down straight into Lily's trembling hands.

'A mirror!' she gasped. Lily ran her finger around the diamond-encrusted rim. 'Oh! It's beautiful.'

'Ahhh, but this mirror,' Benjamin-bat began, 'is no ordinary mirror. My gift has the power to reflect back to you whatever you are feeling: joy, bliss, delight, ecstasy, happiness. Whatever you are feeling will instantly explode inside your head a thousand times stronger.' The bat swung around the light twice before standing upright again. 'Happiness,' he sang happily, 'is like love. Share it and it increases a thousand-fold.'

'But what if I'm not happy?' asked Lily. 'What if I'm scared when I look in the mirror?'

'Oooh! You don't want to do that!' screeched the bat. 'Because if you do' – he raised one webbed wing and hid his head beneath it – 'something might happen!' he finished ominously.

Clasping the mirror tightly to her chest, Lily sat back down.

'Now, stand up Windy,' the bat commanded. Windy jumped up. 'Why, you're a tiny thing! You're not much bigger than me!' he added, sniggering.

'I'm big enough!' exclaimed Windy, going up on her toes and stretching out her neck. 'If you are going to do something, do it now! My stardust is nearly all zonked out!'

'My, my, what a bossy little fairy you are!'

'Yes, and I'm going to be a dead fairy soon if you don't get on with it!'

Bast hissed, but before she could tell Windy off, the bat said gaily: 'I will put your rudeness down to the ignorance of youth. Here!' The bat opened his mouth wide – and a sizzling cloud of sparkling yellow, green and orange stardust puffed out.

'Atishoo!' Windy sneezed as it sprinkled down and over her head. Instantly, the tip of her wand fizzed and sparked like a lit firework. Everyone stared in admiration at the fresh, new eyes sparkling along the rims of Windy's wings. She stared down at her boots. They were shining bright yellow and over-flowing with golden, sparkling dust.

Windy threw up her arms in delighted surprise. 'Thank you. Oh thank you!'

'Had you been a little more polite,' Benjamin-bat said loftily, 'I might have been even more generous. You have only just enough stardust to get you to the first stardust chamber in the lighthouse at the Groyne, or Father Christmas' rocket, as you fairies know it–but no further. Now, keeping hold of your wand, Windy, hold your hands together, palms up.'

Windy did as she was told and the bat lifted one wing again. Instantly a tiny fan delicately painted with miniature red, white and blue butterflies fluttered out from beneath his wing. Flying up quickly, Windy grabbed hold of it. It felt rice-paper-thin.

'Your gift will help the Nature Spirits of Wind, Water and Fire find more strength to fight the witch's extra-ordinary power. But it is not to be used for anything else. Never meddle in things beyond your understanding. It always brings horror and misery.'

'But we need to fly home!' pleaded Windy, fluttering up a little higher. She hovered right in front of the bat. 'What if Demeanor finds the secret chambers first and steals all the magic stardust?' Windy was really whining now. 'Can't I use the fan's power to magic us all the way home?'

'Break my rule and you don't know what might happen,' Benjamin-bat said darkly. 'You risk unleashing the Northern Tiger. And make no mistake, this is no ordinary animal. Its powers are far beyond your understanding. Now, go away. Your fluttering is making me feel queasy.'

Lily shivered. For one mad moment it looked like Windy was going to continue whining and arguing with the bat. Her body was rigid but her yellow boots were shaking. Tiny green specks in the eyes on her wings had begun to fizz and spark angrily. But to everyone's relief, mumbling 'Bats are crackle-bots!'

she darted away and fluttered down onto Lily's knee. Muttering sarcastically 'Oh, get you, crackle-bot Benji-bat!', she folded her arms crossly and sat down.

'I will speak with you next,' Bast announced suddenly.

'Twit-twoo. Delighted to make your acquaintance again.'

'What is my gift?' asked Bast arrogantly.

'Patience! First, I have something to tell you. Before your journey is over, one of you will die!'

'Are you sure?' gasped Bast.

'You cannot change the Law of Destiny. Demeanor will try to kill you all. And when she has captured her victim, she will force them down into the bowels of the earth before sucking out their blood. It will ooze like soft mud into her dark heart and, when it is full to bursting, she will cough out a hideous red-black sludge that will explode across all the land like an erupting volcano! Then everyone will die!' The bat paused to give a short, light chuckle. 'At least, Demeanor seems to think so. Her powers get stronger every day.'

Lily gasped. Slobberchops slapped his paws over his eyes. Windy hid her face between her knees.

'But that's horrible!' exploded Bast.

'Witches are not known for thinking nice thoughts.'

'You mean, you mean … Demeanor is a vampire as well as a witch?'

89

'Of course! She is the Queen of Witches and Vampires, and she always needs fresh blood!'

'But who is her victim?' asked Bast in a barely audible voice.

Pursing his lips, the bat blew a big, loud raspberry! On and on it went, like air escaping from the biggest balloon in the world. Finally, the bat chuckled. 'Heh! Heh! Only joking! Or maybe not. One will die. But you're not to know who, when, where or why!' The bat chuckled some more, louder and louder, before ending in a little hiccup.

Everyone's face had paled – except Bast's, whose cheeks were bright red and bulging with anger. But she knew better than to argue with the bat, so she stayed quiet.

'Stay alert, Bast,' he continued. 'Drop your guard, and Demeanor will kill all of you, slowly and horribly. You are all in great danger.'

'Then Lily and her dog must stay at home. Our journey is too dangerous for a little girl and her dog.'

'Lily and her companion have already made their choice. Besides, you cannot do this alone.' The bat lifted one wing. 'Here – this Cloak of Invisibility will help you.' Instantly, something silky, red and long slithered out from under his wing. *Whoosh!* It flew up high in the air.

Lily and Windy froze. Slobberchops woofed in delight. *A flying red snake*, he thought, wagging his tail. *Yikes! What fun!*

The bright red cloak swooped back down over Bast and, a second later, her head and body vanished.

'Disguise!' exclaimed Benjamin-bat. 'All of history shouts the importance of the element of surprise. Just think what you can do when you are invisible!'

'Is it true?' asked Bast astonished. She spun round. 'Can you see me, Windy?'

'I can see your tail,' replied Windy, laughing. She spun round to face the window. 'Come on. Let's go!'

With a swish of her paw, Bast swung the cloak out over her tail.

'You've vanished!' Lily exclaimed.

'I'm still here.' Bast crept up behind Slobberchops. 'See!' she said, pinching his bottom.

'Ouch!' howled Slobberchops. 'Stop that!'

'Aha! The companion dog,' exclaimed Benjamin-bat. It was the moment Slobberchops had been dreading. 'Stand up. Lift up your head and look at me.'

Slobberchops didn't want to do one single thing this scary-looking bat asked him to do. Looking up at Lily, his sad eyes pleaded: *Do I have to?*

Lily nodded. 'Do it now Slobberchops,' she urged.

Standing up slowly, he looked at the bat. A few moments passed as the bat stared deep into Slobberchops' eyes.

'I CAN SEE YOUR TAIL,' REPLIED WINDY, LAUGHING.
SHE SPUN ROUND TO FACE THE WINDOW. 'COME ON. LET'S GO!'

'I see you are a loyal and faithful dog,' Benjamin-bat began. Slobberchops pricked up his ears. This was hardly what he expected. 'You would give your life for Lily. Everyone should have such a good, loyal and brave companion like you.' *This is brilliant!* Slobberchops thought, beginning to relax. 'But you have your faults,' the bat continued. 'Still, no-one is perfect – and sometimes even faults can have their uses. What would you like me to give you?'

Slobberchops had no idea what he would like a bat to give him. Apart from Lily and Windy, everyone he had ever met had given him insults or smacks. He looked at Lily – and sighed. Everything he ever wanted was here, right next to him. He looked at Bast, then on to Windy. Windy and her wand. *Yes! A wand like that could be useful*, he thought, wagging his tail excitedly. It looked such fun when Windy waved it about. Lifting his paw, he pointed.

'No, you can't have Windy's wand. You're a dog, not a fairy. Here – you can have this stick instead.' Winking at Lily, the bat lifted his wing again. Instantly, a blue stick the size of a large bone flew out from beneath it and nestled itself between Slobberchops' front paws. Slobberchops let out a long, tired sigh. *Lily gets a magic hand mirror, Bast gets an invisible cloak, Windy gets an amazing fan, and what do I get? A boring old stick!*

As if reading his mind, the bat said, 'Make no mistake, this is no ordinary stick. This is …' His voice rat-a-tatted out the final three words like bullets from a gun: 'The … pong … stick!'

'Huh?'

'Everyone has their own smell, Slobberchops, and your stinky doggie smell is particularly horrible to anyone other than another dog. When you lick the pong stick, that smell will increase a thousand-fold. Everyone and everything you point the pong stick at will instantly fall down flat and pass out. Just think: what a fantastic weapon that will be against Demeanor! But I must warn you, brave companion, you must be very careful who you point it at. Now sit down again, smelly.'

'I don't want a pong stick …' Slobberchops grumbled under his breath.

'Well, that's what you've got,' Benjamin-bat shot back. 'But I am feeling generous today, so I'll make it a bit better for you.'

Slobberchops looked down at his blue stick. Already it was slipping from his grasp. Twisting right round, it popped back up as a bone. But this was no ordinary bone – this was a gigantic, Sunday-joint-sized, juicy bone. Slobberchops' tongue lolloped out and he licked his lips. He was about to give his new bone a long, luscious lick – but quickly changed his mind. Lily was staring at him. And she only did that funny thing with her face when she was annoyed with him.

'Or perhaps not,' Benjamin-bat droned. Twisting round again, the bone returned to its original form as a plain blue stick. *Typical!* Slobberchops thought. *I never get any luck.* Muttering 'I don't like bats. Bats are batty bothersome bullies', he poked the pong stick under his collar and sat back down.

'One more piece of advice for all of you,' commanded Benjamin-bat.

'There are powerful forces at work, so watch out! If Demeanor gets her way, then you are all deeeead!' And with that, the bat swooped down and shot straight through the open window.

'Well!' exclaimed Bast. 'I think we caught Benji-bat in a mischievious mood today,' she said, folding her cloak and sitting on it. 'He's not usually that cranky! Never mind, I'm sure our gifts will help us. Windy, are you ready?'

Windy nodded.

'Now remember, keep calm when you do your spell. None of your chilly-dumwumple-dum business. This must be a proper spell!'

*I feel about as calm as a fairy flying a crackle-bot firecracker*, Windy thought, fluttering up. She waved her wand and, in what she hoped was a commanding voice, ordered: 'Map, up!'

Nothing happened. Bast, Lily and Slobberchops glared at the back of Windy's head.

'I said: *Map, up!*' shouted Windy. 'Nature Spirits,' she said, frantically waving her fan, 'do your stuff!'

Nothing happened.

'What kind of a spell is that? Think. Plan. Act. Have you learned nothing?' snapped Bast. 'You can't bore the map and the Nature Spirits with 'Map, up!' You've got to make it sound interesting. Show a bit of intelligence and culture – or make it funny. Anything but shouting. No-one likes a big mouth.'

Windy gave a little shriek of annoyance. She could feel her cheeks burning. This was *sooo* embarrassing. Trying to do magic with everyone watching was just about impossible. Waving her fan in one hand, her wand in the other, in a voice barely above a whisper, she pleaded: 'Magic map, up – don't tease, up up UP! Pleeease!'

To everyone's surprise, the magic map began to shimmy and jerk. Everyone wobbled. Grabbing hold of the sides, Bast just managed to force herself upright. Slobberchops splayed out his legs, whining pitifully. Only Lily was enjoying it. Her eyes were like saucers. So what if she was wobbling like jelly on a plate? Soon she would be flying!

# CHAPTER SEVEN

'**W**atch it, Slobberchops! Mind you don't poke Lily in the eye with your pong stick. It's sticking too far out of your collar. Push it in a bit. Go on. Now!'

*I don't like cats. Cats are catty … and Bast is a busy-body-bossy-boots*, Slobberchops thought, giving the pong stick a quick shove. *But Lily seems to like her, so I suppose I should too.*

The map did a little shimmy, spun round until it was facing the wall, then jerked to a stop. To cheer everyone up, Lily pulled a bag of jelly beans from her pocket. 'Would anyone like a sweetie?' she asked, popping a red jelly in her mouth.

'Really, Lily?!' scoffed Bast. 'This is serious business – not sweetie time! Everyone look straight ahead. It will help Windy concentrate.'

'Um … Bast … Why are we facing the wall? Aren't we going to fly out the window?' asked Lily innocently.

'A wall will help us focus. Windy's done her spell – sort of. Now keep looking at the wall and get the picture of Father Christmas' rocket at the Groyne vividly and very clearly in your mind. Have you all got it?' Lily nodded enthusiastically. Slobberchops too

– although he wasn't quite sure what he was nodding at. 'Good. Now. All we have to do is imagine our map flying us there.'

A few moments passed while eight eyes stared straight ahead. Lily was so nervous she flung her arms around Slobberchops' neck and squeezed. In fact, she hugged so tight, he almost gagged. Slowly but surely, the map hovered up to the height of Lily's bed – and stayed there. Bast sighed with relief, Lily clapped her hands together delightedly and Slobberchops yelped in astonishment. But Windy couldn't believe her luck. 'Magic, magic map,' she chanted, 'fly me straight and true. Do as I ask and … and … I will always love you!'

'What-ho!' the map trilled excitedly. 'Here we go, go, go!' And then, shooting suddenly forward, it whammed straight into the wall.

'Ooooops!' exclaimed Windy.

'Oh!' screamed Lily.

'Are you all right, Lily?' barked Slobberchops.

'I … I think so.'

But Bast had suffered the biggest knock. She had been sitting at the back, and like falling dominoes, everyone had bashed into her, sending her whizzing across the room. She had landed in an ungainly heap under the window. Dusting herself down, she glared across at Windy. 'Everyone sit back on the map!' she commanded through gritted teeth.

Lily, Windy and Slobberchops scrambled back onto the map. Sitting up regally at the back again, the cat licked her paw twice. Taking a deep breath, she ordered: 'Wave your wand, Windy, and I will do the next spell. A proper one, this time – not one that turns Lily's bedroom into a junk yard or smashes us crash-bang-wallop into a wall!'

Windy stabbed the tip of her wand on the map angrily. 'No! I can do it! I can,' she cried, stamping her boots. 'Just give me a moment to think.' Trying to calm herself, she took a long, deep breath, but it just made her feel queasier. If only there was a magic spell to help her do magic spells! *I can do this, I know I can do this, I can – I can!* she told herself. She held up her wand and waved it.

'Get on with it, Windy,' hissed Bast. 'We've no time to waste.'

'I have to be back by morning,' Lily said politely. 'Or Mummy will be very cross.'

'We will be travelling in mind time, Lily. When we want to achieve our goal, mind time is the most precious time of all. It's much better than clock time. And don't worry, Lily, for your clock time has stopped.'

'How?'

'Look at your clock. What time is it?'

Lily looked up at the big pink elephant clock on her bedroom wall. The little hand was on the six, and the big hand went straight up. 'Six o'clock.'

'That's right. Now, keep looking.'

Lily and Bast stared up at the clock. They stared in total silence for what seemed to Lily an awful long time. Suddenly, she exclaimed: 'It's not moving!'

Bast nodded. 'That's right. Now all you need to know is that it's six o'clock now, and it will still be six o'clock on your return. Your parents will never even know you have been away. Benjamin-bat has stopped clock time for you.'

*They will never know*, Lily thought and smiled.

'Now, Windy,' Bast continued solemnly. 'Think. Plan. Act. This time we want proper magic!'

Windy turned to face the wall. In a slightly faltering voice, she began to sing:

*Winds of Nature, weave your way.*
*Fly us to the Groyne today.*
*A smarter cat you'll never find,*
*Than Bast who's wise and sometimes kind.*
*Lily's here too, to show the way:*
*She's sweet and kind, but no-one's fool.*
*I have the magic, and she is the jewel.*
*So fly us away, Slobberchops too.*
*He's Lily's dog, loyal and true.*
*Up magic carpet, up and away!*
*Fly us to the Groyne today!*

Everyone cheered and clapped as Windy finished her spellbinding song. Turning around to face them, she did a quick curtsy and then, smiling coyly, she bent her knee in a slow, low bow. In fact, she bowed so low every single eye on her wings winked. And as the tips clipped the carpet, they crackled and sparked like fireworks.

*Wharooosh!* The magic map shot up so fast Windy fell straight back onto her bottom. Slobberchops let out a howl of surprise. The map swung round quickly. Instinctively Bast swung a protective paw around Lily's shoulder, and Lily had just enough time to catch her reflection, pale and scared, as the map flashed through the open window. A moment later, though, as the wind smacked her cheeks and the fresh night air whistled through her flowing hair, she was clapping her hands and laughing. Her third wish had been granted! They were soaring up higher and higher. It was all BIG beautiful magic!

'Not so fast!' yelled Bast. 'We're flying too high!'

'Faster, faster!' screamed Lily. Leaning over the side, she stared down. They were whizzing over an old Roman fort called Arbeia! It looked so strange – like a giant unfinished jigsaw. 'There's the Little Haven!' she shouted excitedly. 'And that broken down old building is Tynemouth Priory!' she shouted again, pointing. 'And that's … my daddy!' And she was right. There, scurrying and dodging about amongst the ruins, was

'NOT SO FAST!' YELLED BAST. 'WE'RE FLYING TOO HIGH!'

Mr Bloom. Lily's surprise quickly turned to panic. What if he looked up and saw her? He would run home and tell Mummy. She would tell him to stop drinking so much. Then she'd hit him over the head with a saucepan.

'Don't worry,' said Bast, as if reading her thoughts. 'Mr Bloom can't see us – he's not a believer.'

'He can! He can!' screamed Lily. 'Look! He's looking up at us!'

Bast shook her head sagely. 'He's not a believer,' she repeated trying to calm Lily's fears. 'Wave your wand again, Windy. We need to fly down now. And keep your eyes open for the witch.'

Windy waved her wand. Everyone gripped the sides of the map – 'Yikes! What fun!' yelped Slobberchops as the magic map swooped down. When they were hovering little more than a foot above a clump of trees, Windy waved her wand once more. The flying map steadied itself.

'Bast,' Lily asked. 'How did you know Daddy couldn't see me?'

'Mr Bloom has grown too old to believe. Sometimes you might get a shivery knowingness. It might come as a sudden shaft of light through the clouds. Sometimes it's a familiar smell, a gust of wind or a light, feathery touch on your skin that seems to come out of nowhere. The fairies call it shadow-lighting.

Shadow-lights are things you can't see, but you know are there.'

'Shadow-lights …' repeated Lily, astonished. 'I've felt shadow-lights lots of times.' Her voice dropped to a whisper: 'Were they the fairies?'

'Oh, yes, Lily. Every child comes into this world with their very own guardian fairy watching carefully over them … Being born is big magic, and then as children grow every day is a magical day – until one day an adult comes along and tells them it is not! Right now, you have Windy and you have me. Now, stop all your questions, and enjoy!' Flying just above the top of the treetops, Lily felt a brilliant burst of wonderment and happiness surge through her. It was unlike anything she had ever felt before – better than hot chocolate at bedtime. Better, even, than the stories Miss James read to her class, or the shiny gold stars she stuck on Lily's coat for being kind and helpful in class.

They were flying dangerously close to the treetops now. Reaching out Lily could almost touch them with her fingertips. Windy waved her wand again. Whistling merrily, the map soared up then, levelling out, steadied itself.

'Lily!' yelped Slobberchops alarmed.
'You're trembling!'

'It's a little bit scary. You do know don't you? We might never see our home ever again.'

'Don't worry,' Slobberchops said cheerily. 'All roads lead to home eventually!'

Lily giggled, 'Silly Slobberchops!' And then she relaxed. After all, she told herself, this was the magical journey she had wished for. And now, thanks to Benji-bat, it was coming true. And wherever the magic took her, it was her wish, her journey, and it was going to be … amazing!

Leaning far over the edge of the map, watching the twinkling lights in the houses below flash past, Lily's heart now soared somewhere between happiness and paradise! Her three wishes were coming true. She could walk like everyone else. She had two new best friends. She had a magic mirror to help her on her journey. And now she was flying! – She flung her arms around Slobberchops' neck and gave him a great big kiss. His fur felt soft and warm and as cuddly as a teddy bear. She hugged him closer still, and his eyes rolled up as he sighed with happiness and delight.

Standing at the head of the flying map, Windy inspected her pretty fan, turning it over and over in her hands. Sitting bolt upright at the back, Bast purred with pride – and relief. Evil Demeanor, that wicked blood-seeking witch, seemed far, far away.

Five minutes later, Bast was screeching like an alleycat. 'Quick! Quick! Fly down!' Her sharp cat's eyes had seen a shadowy figure in the far distance. It was shooting towards them – too fast to be a cloud.

Everyone gripped the sides as the map swooped down: fast and silent.

As the map levelled off, Slobberchops' nostrils twitched and he gagged. A pungent fog like a big bag of poo had wafted over from the shadowy shape. Jumping up, he let out a long howl of disgust.

'Look, Lily!' he barked, waggling a claw at the dark shape hurtling towards them. 'It looks like a slimy black bag – with something angry and horrible jumping around inside!'

'The witch!' gasped Lily.

Windy waved her wand furiously. Unfortunately for everyone, when she opened her mouth, what came out was not the 'Wicked witch be gone!' she had meant to shout, but an over-excited screech. The wand had no idea what 'Witcheeegeeeooooeee!' meant, so rather than make a wild guess, it did nothing.

'You fools!' a voice shrieked from inside the mysterious shape.

*Bang!* The bag exploded. Lily clapped her hands over her eyes and everyone ducked as thousands and thousands of wooden splinters shot out in all directions. Then, as if drawn by a giant magnet, with a *whoosh* they clapped back together again.

'Yikes!' barked Slobberchops. 'Is that a flying broomstick?' Gliding noiselessly alongside them, less than a foot away, was a long wooden stick. A clumpy tangle of smaller sticks poked out from one end.

*Snap! Crackle!* The twigs split apart. To everyone's horror, a black-robed creature with a hood crawled out! A hooky nose with a red wart on the end jutted out of the hood.

'The witch!' screamed Lily again.

'It's Demeanor!' shrieked Windy, dropping her wand.

'Well!' Demeanor spat, 'if it isn't Windy. The young fairy who can't do her spells! You put your silly little wand up against me, Demeanor, Grandmaster of the Fairies and the entire Underworld?! Ha! Ha! Ha!' she cackled. 'You fools!' Straddling her broomstick, she looped-the-loop just above Windy's head. 'I think I will play a little game with you all before I kill you. Why not? I've waited a long time for this, I could wait a little longer while we play together. It will be such fun!' Hovering over Slobberchops' head, she continued: 'Dog – you can be first. I like a bit of tasty dog!' Swooping down, she clamped her jaws onto Slobberchops' shoulder, bit out a chunk of him and chewed!

'Owwww!' he howled.

'Ugh!' the witch exclaimed, spitting out the lump. 'You taste disgusting! On second thoughts, I think I'll keep you alive. You will be my slave. Royal cats are much more to my taste … Ha! Ha! Ha!' she laughed wickedly once more and, swivelling round, she pointed her broomstick at Bast.

**SNAP! CRACKLE!** THE TWIGS SPLIT APART.

Bast jumped back, hitting out wildly, but it was hopeless. The problem was this: everything about her – from her flowing black robes, Dracula teeth, ugly nose and pimpled hairy chin – shouted *witch*! But there was something extra witchey about Demeanor. She might look like your regular picture-book variety, but as everyone soon realised, she most definitely wasn't.

'Stop it!' Lily yelled, jumping up and hitting out with her fists.

'Little girl, petrify!' screeched the witch. Instantly Lily felt her left leg stiffen as if encased in a block of ice. Then her whole body froze in horror. It was as if the leg brace had swung out of nowhere and clamped itself onto her leg again!

'Ha! Ha! Mmmm! A nice juicy cat for my supper!' Demeanor spat. Leaning across from her broomstick, she jabbed a bony finger at Bast's neck – and missed. Quick as a flash, Bast's right paw caught Demeanor smack on the wobbly wart at the end of her hooky nose. With a *pop*, the nose bounced off, spun round and *popped* straight back on again! Bast swung out bravely again. This time, her paw hit the witch right between the eyes. It was like a stone hitting water: Demeanor's face splatter-gunned into a thousand tiny globules of skin spinning out in all directions.

'Skin, listen to my spell!' shrieked Demeanor's skeletal face. 'Return whence you came – or we all go to hell!' Instantly, the skin globules sprang back onto her skeleton. Sort of. From the tip of her high forehead to her long, pointed chin, Demeanor's face was a mass of fizzing, bubbling warts.

Suddenly, lunging across, Demeanor grabbed Bast by her shoulders – and heaved. Instantly, Bast's back feet were cycling in thin air.

'I have you now!' cackled Demeanor, tightening her grip. 'Roasted cat on toast with a sprinkling of chilli pepper for breakfast! Yummy!'

They were flying higher and higher. Demeanor was straddling her broomstick, riding it like a rocket, with Bast now swinging out helplessly below. With a sinking heart, she stared down at the ground. Lily, Windy and Slobberchops were just about visible. So the bat had told the truth! 'One will die!' he had warned. *I just never thought it would be me,* thought Bast sadly. *Even if I escape Demeanor's clutches, I'll never survive a fall from this height. So I'm 'the One!' But at least my death means my friends will live.*

Staring down, Bast saw something that made her heart almost jerk to a stop: her feet had vanished! A terrible thought flashed through her head. *Had the witch bitten them off?* She glanced up at Demeanor– the witch's warty face stared straight ahead. Bast looked down again. Now, her legs were disappearing too! Instinctively, Bast locked her knees together. Something soft rubbed between them. She wriggled, saw a flash of red, and then the something slithered up her body until she could feel it tickling her shoulders. Her magic cloak! Perhaps she could slip it over her head? If Demeanor couldn't see her, she might think she had escaped and loosen her grip. Death by falling had to be better than death at Demeanor's evil hands – right?

Wriggling her shoulders, Bast took a deep breath, then another, then another. 'Stop wriggling!' shrieked Demeanor, tightening her grip. 'There's no escape. And I have great plans for you before I enjoy eating you!'

'You'll have to find me first!' hissed Bast.

Glancing down, Demeanor nearly fell off her broomstick. Bast's head stared back up at her–and nothing else! This was BIG magic, and it wasn't coming from her! The shock was too much for the witch and she released her grasp.

*How will Windy find her way home without me?* Bast thought sadly as she hurtled towards certain death.

'Quick! Wave your wand, Windy,' yelled Lily.

Windy waved her wand, round and round, up and down, up and down, back and round – but it was hopeless.

'Not enough stardust!' Windy screamed desperately. 'We're falling and the witch is catching us up!'

'Use your magic fan, Windy!' Lily screamed.

Windy held up her fan and waved it frantically over her head. It was just as if she had switched on a giant wind machine. The sudden mega-blast from the fan whooshed its way up and around and … blew Demeanor right off her broomstick.

'Be gone, witch!' shouted Windy. It would be difficult to say which was the louder: the Wind Spirit's jubilant howl of triumph or Demeanor's howl of rage as the second sudden gust of wind hit her full in the stomach. Whistling merrily like a train shooting down a long, long tunnel, the Wind Spirit hurled the witch back, back, back and into the far distance.

'Winds of Nature, save Bast!' Windy shouted, frantically waving her magic fan again.

*Whoosh!* The Wind Spirit captured Bast's legs in a tight whirlwind – and tugged!

'Look out!' shouted Bast as she plummeted towards them. 'I'm going to crash into you. Out of the way!'

'Quick, Slobberchops,' yelled Windy, giving his bottom a slap. 'Stick out your tail!' Instantly, Slobberchops jumped up and wagged his tail. *Yikes! This is so much fun!*

'Keep it still, Slobberchops!' Lily said urgently. 'Bast can't grab hold!'

But Slobberchops couldn't keep his tail still. In fact, he was so excited, it whizzed round faster still. But it didn't matter. The Wind Spirit positioned the cat so well she still managed to grab a hold. And seconds later, she had hauled herself back onto the flying map.

'LOOK OUT!' SHOUTED BAST AS SHE PLUMMETED TOWARDS THEM.
'I'M GOING TO CRASH INTO YOU. OUT OF THE WAY!'

'Oh Bast!' Lily exclaimed, flinging her arms around the cat's neck, 'I thought the witch had deaded you!'

Panting heavily, 'She almost did!' Bast blurted out.

'We beat the witch!' Windy squealed, fluttering around Bast's head. 'We beat the witch!'

Slobberchops face beamed with pride and happiness – even though his tail now felt as if it was about to drop off, he'd rescued the cat and made Lily and everyone happy – right? Like soldiers after a magnificent hard-fought battle, everyone felt relieved – as well as utterly exhausted.

Windy fluttered up to Lily's shoulder. Settling down, she hugged her knees tightly. Lily rubbed her left leg and wiggled her toes. The witch was gone, and now her leg was changing back to normal. But the really puzzling thing was that even before the witch had vanished, Lily had told herself she could beat the witch's spell – she must – and she did! When the witch had screeched 'Petrify!' casting her wicked spell, Lily had frozen. It was just as if her leg brace had clamped itself onto her left leg again. But then *I can do this*, she had said to herself over and over, *I can do this. I can. And I will!* As if by strong magic her left leg had moved, just a little, but enough for Lily to know the strength of her will had definitely broken the spell. 'I faced my fear and did it anyway,' she whispered to herself. 'I was brave!' she added laughing. She leaned back on Slobberchops. And, after a bit of shuffling, Bast gave up and allowed Slobberchops to lean back and lay his head in her lap.

The immediate danger was over. The broomstick had crashed to the ground and Demeanor the witch (propelled along by ever-stronger gusts of wind from the Wind Spirit) was nowhere to be seen.

The magic map flew on. Too exhausted even to speak now, everyone's head buzzed with the same scary question. How long and how far would the Wind Spirit blow and keep the wicked witch away? Everyone that is, except Slobberchops. He was reliving the moment the cat had finally caught hold of his tail. Lily had looked so happy. What a wonderful adventure they were all having!

The map flew on and the sky grew darker. Sitting bolt upright at the back, Bast's tail whipped around restlessly. In fact it whipped so far and so fast, it nipped and clipped Slobberchops around his head several times! Sighing loudly, he crawled around Lily – and slumped down in front of her. Lily patted his back and gently stroked his neck. Sitting cross-legged at the head of the map, Windy flipped her magic fan over and over in the palm of her hand. It seemed their scary thoughts shooting like fiery sparks through their heads, would keep them wide awake forever. When sleep finally came it was deep, far too deep, and long, far too long.

It was as if Demeanor had crept out from the darkness and cast a spell over all of them.

# CHAPTER EIGHT

'Wake up, everyone – we've flown off course!' exclaimed Bast. 'We've all slept too long! Lily, wake up. Where are we?'

Yawning widely, Lily leaned out over the edge of the map and stared down. She shook her head. 'I'm not sure. That way,' she said, pointing, 'is the Roman wall, and past those …' she nodded towards some mountains shrouded in grey mist, '… are the Cheviots. There it is!' she exclaimed, pointing down at the huge crumbling building. 'Tynemouth Priory. We saw it before, remember?' She swallowed hard. 'Just before we saw the witch.'

Everyone leaned over the edge of the map. They had all woken up to hot sunshine beaming down from a clear blue sky. Windy smiled. She thought it a good omen. Putting a hand up to her eyes, she stared down at the priory, thirty or more feet below. 'We've been flying in circles – and for quite a long time.' She turned to Bast. 'I know I should have said this last night, but I was tired and I forgot. I think you should thank Slobberchops. He saved your life!'

Slobberchops pricked up his ears. A light was flickering on in his brain. Was it true? Was the high and mighty cat about to thank him?

'Thank you,' muttered Bast.

Yes! Yes! *Kerching kerchang wham bam!* (Things were firing about in Slobberchops' brain. The light of happiness had never shone brighter.) This was better than the biggest juicy bone. In fact, it was better than the biggest, juiciest bone in the whole wide world.

'For wagging your tail…' Bast added, smiling wryly.

There was something in the curve of that smirk that told Slobberchops it wasn't a real thank you. It was… what? It was puzzling, but that sort of thing happened to him lots of times. Lily had given it a funny name he couldn't quite remember. Nevermind, he had enjoyed the moment anyway. Once, a long time ago, when he was a puppy, something small and black with webbed wings had lifted up his earflap and whispered into his ear. *'Being intelligent isn't the most important thing in life.'*

'Then what is?' he had asked.

*'Being kind,'* the voice answered mysteriously. *'Kindness moves mountains,'* the voice had added, which was even more puzzling.

'Lily,' Bast said with sadness in her voice. 'Windy and I have something to tell you.'

Lily turned to face her.

'It is time for you to go home!'

'LILY,' BAST SAID WITH SADNESS IN HER VOICE. 'WINDY AND I HAVE SOMETHING TO TELL YOU.'

'No!' Lily squealed. 'Why? Haven't I been good – and helpful? I was brave, wasn't I? I tried to be as brave as I could,' she added in a small voice.

'You were brave Lily. Windy and I created the magic, but *you* were the only one who made it happen. We could never have got this far without you.'

'Please don't leave me. I don't want to be alone.'

Bast smiled kindly. 'Windy and I are tied to you with bonds of love Lily. You will never be alone ever again. But clock time can only be stopped for twenty-four hours at a time. You must go back now, or everything we have learned, and everything we have achieved so far, will be lost. Forever.'

Fifteen minutes later, the map was see-sawing over the chimneypot on Lily's house.

'See Lily,' Slobberchops yelled wagging his tail. 'I was right. All roads lead to home!'

'Tally-ho!' the map sang merrily. 'We've come far, now here we are!' For one terrible, panicky moment, Lily thought the map was going to whoosh down the chimney, and she would have to climb into bed covered in soot, and there would be black footprints on the white carpet and, and – Mummy would be sooooo cross!

Without warning, the map swerved down and around.

They hovered outside the lounge window. Mrs Bloom was perched on the edge of the white sofa.

Seated opposite, clutching a big black briefcase, was a man as thin as a bootlace.

'They can't see me,' Lily whispered. She giggled. But what Lily heard next nearly had her crying.

'Doesn't surprise me,' Mrs Bloom was saying, 'that Billy Moonface is always up to no good.'

The bootlace man cleared his throat noisily. 'So, you see, Lily will not be on her own at Wratchet's Boarding School.' He reached inside his top pocket and pulled out a scrunched up piece of paper. 'Now if you'll just sign here. I'll make sure Lily's out of your hair as quick as you can say "good riddance".' He did a little cough behind his hand before adding cheerily, '…I mean "goodbye"– just my little joke!'

Mrs Bloom reached into her cardigan pocket and pulled out a white hanky. Raising it above her head, she waved it about like a tiny flag of surrender. 'Oh, you are naughty!' she trilled.

Lily wiped a tear from her eye. Mummy was sending her away to some awful boarding school. Billy Moonface was going to be there too! And Slobberchops? He would never leave her side. Perhaps he could wear Bast's Cloak of Invisibility? Lily looked at Windy, then at Bast. It had been an amazing adventure. But would she ever see her special friends again? Suddenly, she felt her eyelids dropping slowly and deliberately like long, heavy curtains.

CLUTCHING A BIG BLACK BRIEFCASE, WAS A MAN AS THIN AS
A BOOTLACE.

'You will come back. You will return for me, won't you? You promise?'

'I promise,' said Bast. 'When the time is right, we can all call on Benjamin-bat again – and Windy and I will come back for you. This part of our journey together is over, but really it's not the end, it's just the end of the beginning.'

'We will all return,' Bast and Windy whispered in unison.

'And Slobberchops?'

'And Slobberchops. He can bring his pongy pong stick too, if he wants. I have a feeling on our next journey, he'll get to use it!' Bast added smiling.

'And clock time will stop again?'

Bast and Windy nodded.

Lily held her mirror in the palm of her hand. 'I didn't even get to use my magic mirror. Please – can I keep it?'

'You can try,' Bast said with a wink.

*My mirror is magic*, Lily thought, giving it a squeeze. *I must hold on!* The mirror felt cool and smooth.

Lily held the mirror a long time, tracing her finger around the edge. Stroking, patting and flipping it over and over in her palm, she played with it until one-by-one, she felt her fingertips soften smoothing easily into the warm, pulpy metal.

'Always remember Lily,' Bast said, her voice lilting softly, 'you are braver than you believe, stronger than you could ever imagine. And even while we are apart we will always be with you. After all, we have our beautiful bonds of love tying us together – and they will keep you brave and strong.'

Lily blushed. *So Bast thought she was brave!* 'Do you reeeally think I am brave?' she asked astonished.

'But of course!' Bast replied with a chuckle. 'After all, you fought a witch!' The cat paused for a moment. In a slower more serious voice she continued: 'Life is an amazing adventure when you choose it to be – as you did Lily. Adventure requires guts … it requires bravery. You will get hurt, that's all part of an adventurous life! But if you are smart you will learn from your scars.' The cat paused again, this time to smile at Lily. It was a beaming smile bursting with pride. 'You my gutsy little warrior girl,' she purred, 'are as brave as the bravest cat there ever was! And believe me when I say,' the cat winked mischieviously, 'I know what I am talking about!'

Suddenly, a shifting dreamy kind of tiredness swept over Lily's face and then down her body like a dark wandering cloud. For one fleeting moment Lily thought she must be back in her bedroom already, hiding from her mum under her duvet.

'Do I really have to go home now?' she asked in a small sad voice. She could feel her heart pounding against her ribcage, fast and furious, like the hooves of a run-a-way horse. Very soon she would be back in her bedroom again – and while she slept her magical friends would vanish. Her next thought almost had her heart galloping out of her chest. *What if her magical friends never came back for her?*

'I'm not going home!' Lily insisted, panicking.

'You're not?' Windy said astonished.

'No. I'm not! I'm going to stay awake and … and … and fly with you and Bast. Forever!' Lily finished defiantly.

'One day, perhaps. But not this day,' Bast said kindly but firmly. The corners of her mouth turned up in a mysterious smile as she added, 'Your journey is one amongst many. There are more strange events, more magical things in the universe, just waiting to happen. All it takes is the beautiful mind of a child, a delightful dollop of bravery, and belief!'

Stretching her neck, the cat stared up at the stars, and Lily joined her gaze. Windy looked up too, then Slobberchops. At that very moment a streak of glittering light swept across the sky from one side to the other.

'A shooting star!' squealed Windy.

Bast smiled. 'That's Benjamin-bat's way of saying you can have a parting wish Lily. But you mustn't tell us what it is. Everyone close their eyes now while Lily makes her wish.'

*One more wish!* Lily closed her eyes and silently made her wish. It was a beautiful shared moment full of wonder that Lily would remember forever.

Suddenly Lily felt a big hot tear pop out of the corner of her eye and roll down her cheek.

Lifting Slobberchops' earflap she whispered, 'I mustn't tell you what I wished for, but best friends always keep their promises, don't they?'

Windy darted up. Fluttering her wings, with the tip of her wand she gently traced two large heart-shapes on Lily's forehead, one above each eye. Lily decided then and there never to wash her forehead ever again.

'Thank you Windy,' she said shyly. 'I have to be brave now and say goodbye don't I?'

'Not goodbye. Au revoir Lily. Au revoir means until we see each other again. But for the magic to work you have to really, really believe that Bast and I will come back for you.' Going up on tip-toe, she twirled around in a circle. 'Then we will!'

Without thinking about what she was doing Lily yawned. It was a big wide yawn, and the cool early evening air tingled across her tongue – before suddenly shooting right up her nose! Lily was sure it was the same magical air she had gulped in at the very beginning of her adventure. 'Thank you Wind Spirit,' she whispered.

'You're welcome,' the Wind Spirit breezed back to her – although Lily thought it sounded a lot like Benjamin-bat's voice.

'Lily, it is time,' Bast said softly. 'Look at me. Look deep into my eyes.'

Lily stared at the cat's eyes. They had changed. Now it was like looking down two long dark tunnels, at the very end of which two bright green specks twinkled and winked – like swinging lanterns – calling – luring her in. And the longer Lily stared, the more she felt the distant less-enchanted world they called from, draw closer and closer.

'Bast,' she whispered, 'I will have to wear my brace again now, won't I?' Lily couldn't be sure (just a single sliver of light peeped out now from beneath the curtain of darkness that was falling), but just before Bast's eyes closed, she glimpsed that same sad, distant look she had seen once before.

The last thing Lily saw was Windy standing up on tiptoe, stretching out her arms. Every eye except one on her beautiful wings had closed, as if they were fast asleep. Lily smiled. Had the Wind Spirit sprinkled everyone with magic sleeping dust?

The one open eye on Windy's wings winked at her, and then it, too, closed. *I am going to remember this*, Lily thought. *Every magical bit. I am … I really, really am … Benji-bat, and Bast and Windy … I am … I am …*

'Benji-bat …' she mumbled under her breath.

Barely above a whisper, Lily heard, 'Benjamin-bat, at your service. No job too big, no job too small, just give …' And then he too faded, and she heard nothing, nothing at all.

As the darkness closed in, Benji-bat, Bast, Windy and finally the magic flying map softened and melted like freshly poured milk into steaming hot chocolate. In her mind, Lily heard Bast and Windy whispering once more: *We will all return*. And then Lily knew, she just knew, she was about to dream the most exciting, the longest, the most dangerous and definitely the most amazing dream she had ever had.

Lily stared up at the big pink elephant-shaped clock on her bedroom wall. 'The little hand is still on six,' she whispered, 'and the big hand is straight up. Six o' clock!' she squealed triumphantly. So it was true: Benji-bat had stopped clock time!

'It's never-ending magic!' Lily exclaimed excitedly, giving Slobberchops a great big hug.

And it was.

'IT'S NEVER-ENDING MAGIC!' LILY EXCLAIMED EXCITEDLY, GIVING
SLOBBERCHOPS A GREAT BIG HUG.

FLY WITH LILY AND HER MAGICAL FRIENDS AGAIN ON
ANOTHER EXCITING AND DANGEROUS ADVENTURE

# LILY, WINDY AND THE WITCH:
# THE JOURNEY CONTINUES

will be available late 2016.
If you would like to find out the latest news,
please visit the website:
www.lilywindyandthewitch.co.uk

For further information visit:
www.lilywindyandthewitch.co.uk

Books for adults
www.yvonnecarlinpage.co.uk